Also by Guichard Cadet

LoneWolf's Cry
0-9647635-0-8; Feb. 1996

The Masks of Flipside
0-9647635-4-0; May 1998

Bard From Par Taken
0-9718191-0-6; June 2002


Other La Caille Nous titles

Separate but Equal
0-9718191-4-9; Sept. 2002

Backfield in Motion
0-9718191-3-0; Aug. 2002

When He Calls
0-9647635-9-1; June 2002

Father's Footsteps
0-9718191-1-4; June 2002

Water in a Broken Glass
0-9647635-7-5; Sept. 2000

When You Look At Me
0-9647635-6-7; June 2000

Temples
0-9647635-5-9; Feb. 1999

Party Ain't Over Yet!
0-9647635-3-2; March 1997

The A# Blu's
0-9647635-2-4; Sept. 1996

My Baby's Father
0-9647635-8-3; April 2001 (revd.)

# THE CANON OF LOOSE CANNONS

# THE CANON OF LOOSE CANNONS

Guichard Cadet

LA CAILLE NOUS

Edited by Marie Michael

Cover Illustration & Design by Austin Greene


Cadet, Guichard, 1968-,
    The canon of loose Cannons / Guichard Cadet.
        p. cm.
    ISBN 0-9718191-2-2 (pbk.)
        I. Title.

PS3553.A31345 C36 2002
813'.54--dc21                                    2002024005


La Caille Nous Publishing Company, Inc.
PO Box 1004
Riverdale, MD 20738
www.lcnpub.com

Media & Distribution
328 Flatbush Avenue, Suite 240
Brooklyn, NY  11238
212-726-1293

*In memory of*
*Kenny Caldwell*

Donate to support the Kenny Caldwell Scholarship Fund, which gives financial assistance to students from West Philly and Our Mother of Sorrows (Kenny's grade school) who show academic promise and financial need.

The Kenny Caldwell Scholarship Fund
c/o The Philadelphia Foundation
1234 Market Street
Philadelphia, PA 19102

# THE CANON OF LOOSE CANNONS

# THE CANON OF LOOSE CANNONS

*"My enemy's friend is my enemy."*

*"My enemy's enemy is not necessarily me."*

# The Mor'al Majority

Austin Malleron stands in front of his farmhouse and stares up at the sky. The sky resembles an ocean being navigated by a large ferry filled with screaming passengers. It is as if a hijacking were taking place. A small number of clouds are bunched up, and another group is scattered all over the place, as if claiming to be separate entities. Austin is wearing a blue Osh Kosh farmer-styled jumpsuit. One of the straps is unbuttoned, dangling off his left shoulder, down to his knees. He had promised the family a trip to the amusement park, and today is the day. He does not feel much like going, but fears disappointing the kids. All last summer and early fall he told them to wait for this year's season opening. Now the time has arrived, time to go back to a place he dreaded as a lad. Austin has not been to the amusement park since he was seventeen, the age old man Malleron chose to let his children make their own decisions.

Austin ventures to the barn, to ensure that the station wagon is working properly. He knows the pickup is working, but it is used primarily for errands on or near the farm. After the visual check, he leans his back against the wagon. The amusement park is a two and half hour drive from their home. Thoughts of the day ahead race through his mind: screaming, laughter, gunshots, water. Then the silence that looms once all has left. When he was a youth, he always felt the silence because his father always insisted that their family be the last one to leave, his father's way of making sure they got a chance to enjoy any of the rides they may have missed. Old man Malleron always insisted that he, Austin, the eldest of the children accompany him on all the rides. That was the old man's idea of father and son bonding.

Austin found this idea ludicrous. His father never spoke to him unless it was for disciplinary reasons, on their way up to the peak of the roller coaster, or while going through the *House of Fear*. Because of this lack of communication, Austin promised himself that he would be a totally different type of parent than his father had been. An open line of communication, a hug whenever wanted, or anything to let his children know he was there for them. He even pledged never to force them to the amusement park. Yet, he never expected his children to force him. He thought once grown the days of the *House of Fear* would be in his past. But, one month before this year's opening Sarah and Dennis came home from school and reminded him they wanted to go. They said it as if they were ordering him, yet he put them off. The stall strategy worked until they got Peggy involved. Since he had never told her of his days in Dire County, he couldn't truly explain his aversion to returning to the amusement park.

The barn door opens and slams into his arm. He looks down and sees Brad, the youngest of his three children. Brad runs behind him, cradling his legs as if trying to hide. His rushed and excited words are "they are trying to get me."

He rubs the lad's blond hair then picks him up and asks "Ready for your big day in the park?"

Brad's answer doesn't come. Instead his eyes meet Austin's, allowing the father to see the son's hesitancy. Brad nods then gives Austin a hug. Upon hearing Sarah and Dennis' voices, Brad shrieks "Daddy, put me down, they're after me."

Sarah and Dennis come running out of the house. Their maniacal looks and hurried shouts of "there he is" anger Austin, mainly they remind him of why he is returning to the *House of Fear.* Those two had a way of influencing their mother, which in turn became their way of controlling him. As they approach, Austin commands, "Stop all the noise. Everyone get in the car. It's time."

He starts the automobile and drives to the front of the house where Peggy is standing. Looking at her physique and smile, he realizes he would forever be at Sarah and Dennis' mercy, for Peggy was a beauty. From the first time he met her, as she hitchhiked on backcountry road, she had him going against his instincts. At first she wanted to move back to the town where he grew up because she loved the stories about Dire County. As all others who've never lived there, Peggy called it legend or lore. To Austin, it was reality or simply history, if you wanted it stripped down to some of Dire's harsh truths. So, they compromised and moved as close as he could stomach.

As Peggy gets in the passenger's side, Dennis complains that he should be the one to sit in the front seat. After losing the debate, he starts to complain again. Austin gives him a hard stare and Dennis shuts up. Austin starts the drive by turning on the radio. Sarah and Dennis shout, "Not the oldies station, dad."

"It's not the oldies station. It's good music." Peggy turns the dial to a station she considers a compromise to both sides. Austin defends his choice, "It's music from when people played instruments and knew what music was supposed to sound like."

Austin hears their snickers and looks over his shoulder. Brad is seated quietly between his siblings. Austin notes that Brad has his demeanor and Peggy's looks. Brad seems so distant from all the pushing and screaming Sarah and Dennis are doing across him. To Austin, he seems to be pretending that the flat countryside and the farm animals are his lone focus. But Brad's eyes tell a different story. They stare blankly ahead, as if mesmerized and fearful of the journey, and remind Austin of his first time to the amusement park. The kids at school used to tell of these exciting stories of their visit to the park. The stories only frightened Austin. He had hoped that the amusement park would have proven its worth, once he witnessed and experienced it for himself.

It had not.

The drive nears two hours. All of the children are asleep. Austin has switched back to the oldies station and is tapping his fingers on the wheel. "Drive a little faster. At this rate, we'll never get there." He ignores his wife, and starts to hum along with the tune. The humming and tapping are distractions to keep his mind from drifting into memory lane, where eight years of biannual amusement park mayhem looms. He does not want to think of the time that little Sue Deranson vomited her lunch on the roller coaster's first drop. Nor does he want to think of the time two grown men, from a place he had never heard of, fell off the sticky walls of the ride called *The Hell Hole.*

The hole had been spinning at a high speed. From above, future and past riders watched bodies pinned against the walls, pinned by speed, wind, electricity and desire. When the movement got too fast, it seemed as if the riders' will swayed. They fell off the sticky wall and onto the steady base. Austin had never seen that happen before. Thoughts ran through his mind: Was it their fear? Was something being taken for granted? Something assumed? Out of nowhere two grown men dropped. Their fall linked them with those standing on top and looking down at *The Hell Hole.* For the watchers: breath gasping, voices whispering, noise cackling, laughter escaping. For the fallen: knees bruised, egos tarred, and morale broken. Minutes later, only the memory was left as a token. No harm done.

Austin's worst memories are from later that day. He was sharing a car with the next county's future homecoming queen, a girl rumored to have had a crush on him. When she first asked him to go into the house with her and her family, he saw the visions. Foreshadowing, he just knew that he would end up marrying her. Instead, halfway through the *House of Fear,* Austin let out a loud shriek and his bladder gave way, causing a stream to run down his right leg.

"Are you driving slow because you're scared?" Peggy's voice

shakes him out of his reveries.

"Peggy if you don't shut your mouth..." Austin catches himself sounding like the type of man his father was, and stops mid-sentence. Ever since the *House of Fear* incident, the word scared brought him back as if he was reliving the moment and the teasing he received in its aftermath. That girl told everyone "he was so scared..." and the story became part of Dire's lore.

He looks over at his wife, reaches out and strokes her on the back of the head. She moves closer to him and rests her head on his shoulder. Twenty minutes later they arrive at the parking lot of the amusement park. It is crowded with cars. The children wake. Seeing that they've reached their destination, Sarah and Dennis exit out their side of the car and race to the admission line. They stare into the park, pointing at the numerous attractions and exclaiming, "wow!" at each of the towering rides. Brad waits for his father to come out of the car, grabs his hand and walks him in his mother's direction in order to grab her hand too. As he trots toward the other children, he has a wide smile on his face, showing the security a child feels when both parents are by his side.

The admission line is not long. Once inside, Austin allows the two older children to go as they please with one stipulation, "Return here forty-five minutes before closing time!"

"Can we take Brad with us?" Sarah giggles after the question.

Austin answers in a tone that suggests he does not appreciate the humor in Sarah and Dennis' looks.

Unlike the precise way his father organized the trip to the

amusement park, Austin simply lets everyone go as they please. Sarah and Dennis run toward the towering rides. He and Peggy take Brad to all the kiddie rides, buy him cotton candy, popcorn and drinks. Austin wins him a huge panther after collecting points at the water shooting gallery, duck hunt, and coin toss.

Whereas the morning had a brisk spring wind, the afternoon is pleasant, with temperatures in the low seventies. There isn't much wind. As they make their way around the park, Austin greets the many who recognize him, but doesn't linger too long. Until running into some high school buddies, he had yet to run into any close friends. The many he had seen barely knew his family, but these guys knew him and his past. He had not seen them since leaving Dire County four months after college graduation. Austin introduces Peggy and Brad. The friends are also at the park with their families. Their wives had also been childhood friends or people whose families he knew. They all still live in Dire County, about thirty miles from the park. They are about to chide Austin about the incident in the *House of Fear*, but he quickly changes the topic and compliments them on their families.

When Austin last saw them, only Tommy had children, two of them during college with his high school sweetheart. The men walk away from their families, leaving the wives and children talking to each other. The conversation starts with their days in high school, when they lettered in three sports and held dreams of receiving scholarships to top programs, and eventually leads to why Austin steered them away from his family.

"So, how is it out there?"

"Why do you call it out there?" Austin assumes Tommy is speaking to him.

"Not talking to you Austin." Tommy answers out of the corner of his mouth, talking as if he is chewing on a twig.

Jonathan jumps into the conversation the way a person breaks up a fight between strangers. "I moved out to Seattle a little over a year ago."

"Why?" asks Austin, concerned about why Jonathan would move so far away from the land his great-grandfather helped build.

As if unable to articulate his thoughts, Jonathan uses his hands while speaking. His palms face upward, spreading out only to return closer together. "I needed to leave my past behind."

Austin places his hands on Jonathan's shoulders. "That is exactly why I left."

"Stop lying! You were a coward. A little pussy." With but a breath taken and one blink's notice, Austin hovers Tommy before the last words were out of his mouth. The other men step in and diffuse the situation

Tommy half-apologizes, "Sorry for my choice of words, but you and Jonathan moved for different reasons. His family still lives here. He speaks fondly of this place and encourages others to come see for themselves. You don't. He is like a missionary, trying to expand our tradition and legacy. You are a deserter."

Austin's vacant stare causes Tommy to stop speaking, forcing him to become self-conscious, fully aware of the emotional baggage that he's been carrying. Tommy was the only one who knew Austin was leaving. As they shared a six-pack of beer on a dry, starless August night, Austin told him that he'd sold his family's house. It was a week after serving as the best man in Tommy's wedding. They had never spoken about such things and Tommy felt it was only right that Austin discussed the decision with the other guys. By night's end, Tommy got him to agree to such a group talk. Austin left Dire at sunrise, so he understands why Tommy is still angry.

The men split into two groups. Austin doesn't ask but he wishes Jonathan would walk with him so he could find out why Jonathan really left. Instead Don walks with him. As they stroll in a half-circle back to their families, Austin decides to continue the conversation, hoping that Don would understand why he left. "Why do you stay here?"

"By choice."

"But it's not yours."

Don laughs, "So, that's why you left?" He laughs a bit more then places his right arm around Austin's shoulders. "No man has a choice. Choice is being! If you are not, then you become. Do you get me?"

Austin shakes his head, "I beg to differ."

"Therefore, you're challenging the law of the land."

"How so?"

"That old saying about how beggars couldn't be choosers." They both laugh, acknowledging the sparring session.

Austin tries a new reasoning, "My whole thing is a new beginning. A fresh start."

Don shouts "Impossible!" He then lowers his voice when he notices that a few heads had turned his way. "You can't erase history."

"I understand that. But why does every person feel he has to have his own story. Why can't we have just one story?" Austin's voice cracks, as if begging, a throaty form of despair, like that of a brother seeing a dead sibling walking. There is a legend in Dire County, and Austin knows it well. The dead have appeared from thin air, and disappeared also, which by the way is not as scary to Dire's inhabitants. It is now a common occurrence. It has become the closest closed closet door, so to speak.

Where's your daddy, little girl? *He ran out and left us.*

Hey Sonny, where's your dog? *I dunnno...*

*Yes. Yes, you'll be all right.* Those are the notorious words of Dire's history: forecast, foresee, for play...Everything is there for amusement, even history.

"In this amusement park anything can happen." Austin continues to ramble in order to avoid discussing his most recent thoughts. "A man can lose his focus and begin traveling in circles. That's what I learned here. It's not the history or the place that scares me. It's the things that we have taken for granted and labeled *for play.* Do you know what I mean?"

Don stares away as if hiding a personal story. "Yes. In a way I do."

"Then, how do you handle it?"

"I don't Austin. I just live and let die." He stops walking and adds, "That's all. No need to ask for forgiveness. No sob stories.

That's all."

Austin looks at him, slowing down their pace. "Do you think I came here to ask forgiveness for leaving?"

"Yes. And none of us are angry with you for leaving, except Tommy, but he would also welcome you back. You're always welcome to come back, with your new family." Don laughs as if sensing that Austin's pride is the barrier. "If not for yourself, then come back for your wife and kids. You have this legacy to fall back on, they don't. They need a place to worship the past, and place to recall the good times."

Austin grabs him by the shoulders, seemingly trying to shake sense into him. "How can you laugh in here? People come here and are never seen again."

"You assume those things to be true?"

Don's calm tone and lack of reaction to his grasp causes Austin to take his hands off of him. He sighs. "My entire family came to this amusement park and never returned home."

Don shakes his head, confirming either that he doesn't believe the story, or why Austin would speak of it. "Yes, I remember. That incident resurrected the belief that the dead are amongst the living and that reality is a simple question: Who do you want to be? I remember how at first folks around the county claimed you killed them and disposed all seven bodies without any clues. Tommy stood by you from the beginning. He never believed you killed them."

"That's not the impression I get from him."

"After you left here, the doubts many people had resurfaced."

"It's not like I left the next day. I stayed here for nearly two years." Austin points at him. "What about you?'

"I never believed you killed them and still don't."

Austin had not been to the amusement park for three years, ever since his incident in the *House of Fear*. It was that year's grand opening and Old Man Malleron had fighting words for him because he refused to go. The whole family loaded up and never returned. Though he was the one to call the police, after weeks of investigation, he became the primary suspect. Everyone suspected he had done something to his family. He had to build this emotional wall around himself, yet not draw more suspicion. "Can you believe they investigated me for months and never checked for the bodies here in the park?"

"I still believe they're alive somewhere out there. And, that they left you because they were ashamed because you refused to return to the park after you pissed on yourself."

Austin shakes his head to brush off a remark he could not take when he was younger. "I'm beginning to think that I was an orphan like some claimed when the international media came on the scene."

Austin looks up and spots Peggy and Brad. As the giant wheel whirls its way down, bringing them more clearly into view, he firmly shakes hands with Don, as if reaffirming a truce. Don compliments him on his wife's beauty then kids him about that being the reason Austin left. "Couldn't get a beauty from this county after...?"

"I can still have your wife. In fact, I think I did. Behind the bleachers, high school, junior year, if I'm not mistaken."

Don grimaces, as if wanting to say something, but he remembers the pecking order. Austin and Tommy were always the ringleaders. As Don walks in the opposite direction, he says, "I never took you for the fickle type."

"I'm not coming back. This is a learning experience for the kids."

"Swallow your pride and lose your insecurities before teaching."

The distance between them grows. They are practically shouting.

"Bitter 'cause you chose not to leave the past for the future?"

"Austin, only a fool like you can mistake a new past for the future."

They both smile and say to the other. "I'll see you."


The park is fully ablaze in the wonder that is night. The sky is a grayish mass with an orange flare stretching across the horizon. Families begin to count their members and head out of the park. Laughter is heard in every direction, and screams echo in the northwest corner of the park. Austin guides his wife and child in that direction, knowing it is where Sarah and Dennis are to be found. Although it is more than the forty-five minutes before closing he tells them it is time to leave. Masses of people head toward the parking lot. An old man is running to the exit, his hair fluttering in the wind as if his fingers had touched an open current of electricity. He is yelling, "They're amongst us" over and over.

His steps are rapid and off the given path. His knees buckle to the outer side on every step. It is as if he has been wounded. Spittle runs out of his mouth. Children laugh, babies cry, and parents gather. There isn't a panic, but the crowd moves hurriedly, avoiding contact, making sure no one bumps into anything or anyone. Dennis is pitching a bitch at having to leave before getting the opportunity to enter the house. Sarah joins in, "You're not our father. Earlier I met a man who told me you came three years after I was born. Is that true, Mommy? Is it..."

Peggy asks him to stay a little longer to quiet the kids. Nearly half the crowd has left the park. Those on line for the *House of Fear* have changed their minds.

As if fully schooled on Dire's lore, history if you may, Dennis challenges him, "If you're really our daddy, you'll lead us into the house and give us a past."

Brad stares at the different speakers, amazed by the shouting. He is sucking on his last piece of cotton candy. His face is sticky pink, his eyes wide with innocence. Austin knows the event being played out is beyond Brad's grasp. Brad knows not the test of bastards, the loyalty of carpenters like him who come to fix a broken past, and the harvest of blue moons like Peggy. He had married her because of love and loneliness. After leaving Dire, his life had quickly become an empty road cutting across a canyon. She was working in a mill town, struggling to support two kids, ages three and two. Two different men had left their seed. At first, he thought he knew her type, especially after hot sex in the back of his pickup, her way of thanking him for the ride. Though he told her he was just passing through, she gave him her address and phone number. The next day he called and stopped being a drifter. He had traveled slowly. It had taken him three months to go five hundred miles away. Two years later, they married and agreed to come back closer to Dire, to what she and the older children see as lore.

"I want to go into the house," repeat Sarah and Dennis.

Austin bows to Sarah and Dennis' request. Peggy hugs him firmly. He never thought that his friends' wives and other strangers would be so bold as to run down Dire's history and beliefs, without care for how he might feel about the place. Austin wants to, but doesn't, ask her whether the life he has created for them is not enough.

Sarah and Dennis run ahead to one of the empty cars on the electric railing. The cars hold two each and travel alone. The ride through the house is done as if it were a ritual. The car carrying the head of the family is the last to go through. It is his duty to ensure that all are safe, by being the sacrifice. Every other rider will see popup cardboard monsters, except for the person in this particular car, who is forced to enter the closets of the past. Voices speak rapidly in the dark, and it is up to Austin to identify them. Every Dire County family's history is known. Dire's inhabitants are bound not only to the land, but also to all those who've lived there before them. By leaving Dire, Austin essentially believed he could sever his ties with this land.

He picks up Brad and hugs him tightly, knowing that act alone would have given him more confidence in his own father.

"Remember that the body is only a symbol. Your mind, the voice within, is the guide. I am always with you. I am your father. If tomorrow be bleak and sorrowful, know that it is for you I speak."

"But daddy..."says the lad as if he truly understands and is not willing to risk losing his father.

"My son, forget not my ways, even in days of old."

Peggy snatches Brad out of his arms and places him back on his feet. "You're scaring the boy."

"What do you think, recollecting the past has no consequences?"

Without answering, she cradles Brad's shoulder, motioning him and the other children toward the ride. Austin goes to the entrance reserved for family heads. The entrance is a high black spike fence with a mossy base. It stands in front of a huge lawn. From the distance, he sees the two other cars entering the house. Sarah and Dennis wave as they enter. Brad is clutching Peggy's left hand; she is smiling.

A hooded woman wearing a black robe appears from a passage underneath the grass. Once she is out, the passage door shuts without any assistance. She sits on top of the door, her posture indicating that Austin would have to go through her to enter the house. She beckons Austin, pointing at him with her right index finger then points at the grass. Her fingers exaggerate the movement, indicating below the surface, his burial. A guitar materializes on her lap and she begins strumming a chord. Austin lifts the gate's latch and enters to sit facing her. She introduces herself as the Keeper of the August Moon. Her question is quite simple. "It has been a long time. Why are you back?"

Austin answers by singing the first words of the song of the past. "I was all alone with the ghost of Flipside. A broken man's dream is my life."

She joins in singing the song, and at its end, she bows her head on the final note. He claps once. She lifts her head. Her eyes remind him of a ship lost at sea during a storm. The pupils are the sails. The moisture around them makes it seem as if the wind is blowing them to the corner. The lashes are soaked, reflecting the ship's predicament. Passengers head under for cover. The cargo is cramped, the crew panicking, screaming, *we're not going to make it.* The voice of doom speaks throughout the ship. Cries. Bodies colliding. Mutiny.

His father loved the ceremonial aspect of entering the house, and reveled in always retelling of the keeper's tradition. The keepers are a sect, like priests and nuns to the church. As the keeper spreads her arms rapidly, with all her might and vanishes, a rickety car creeps up on the lawn and stops where Austin stands. Before entering, he checks his surrounding, surveying the place as if he expects to be gunned down if he attempts to sit. He sits. The car picks up speed. It bangs into the house's front door, and heads for the basement. The place is completely dark except for the purple bulbs reflecting off paper skeletons and masked monsters. A creepy laughter echoes throughout the house. Austin also hears shouts, voices arguing and the normal laughter. The house forces recollection, especially of those who'd like to forget. As each car passes through a room, a noise is heard. The traveler's duty is to identify the noise, to show that he knows his family's history. The house then makes a noise or several noises to express the traveler's feelings toward the ancestor. Various noises are made: gunshots, laughter, worship, guillotine, lynching, etc...

He hears a whisper, "Seven rooms to combat Austin. Austin...even if you kill your family, it still is your legacy."

*A baby's cry!* Austin answers, "Impossible." The car is still in the basement. As it exits toward the stairs, he hears claps.

*Pots clanging in a kitchen sink!* "Blue Moon. I saw you..." Cheers, that of voices in a stadium.

In the living room, the car approaches the bookshelf, and quickly spins towards the dividing doors that separate the dining room. The doors split open; the cabinet's door opens, *china falls and forks drop* as the car enters. "Great Uncle Trevor." Chewing, then gulps as if something was being drunk. Austin tosses frantically in the car. He is sweating profusely. The lights come on and the car does not move. There is no one else in the room. The lights go off. The car returns to the living room.

The door of the entertainment system swings open. *The stereo blares Forties blues,* something down home, something Chicago is being blown through the speaker. "Mad Dog Raven, my father's eldest brother." There's a scratching sound. The music of the past is mixed with the present: "Niggaz have been dying for four hundred years..." In the background a chorus of "Ayes" respond to a vote being taken.

The car proceeds upstairs to the second floor and into the master bedroom. The linen on the bed is bloody, yet the bed is made. A canvas shows two nude women with huge breasts and snakes wrapped from their ankles to their upper thighs. Both bedroom closets swing open. *A bomb explodes; Austin hears sobs then cries.* "Mother!!!..." He slides down the car railing and starts to cry. His clothes have become disheveled. A cold sweat runs from his head and down to his body. His stomach turns. He feels the acid in his mouth and tries to hold back, but he vomits over the side of the car. He feels clammy, tries to compose himself then vomits again.

The car plods its way to the bathroom. The room reeks of urine and feces. The medicine chest opens slowly. It contains all kinds of pills. He cries, "Roam, my nigger, my younger brother..." *Gunshots. Blohp, blohp, blohp.* As the car makes its way out of the room, Austin lifts the toilet seat. It's full of green shit. Money green. Vein green. Blood green. The tiles are red. Austin feels blood racing through his body. Sweat pours from his brow. He is breathing heavily. The house is laughing. It is a hysterical laugh, the kind reserved for viewers of Eddie Murphy's *Raw.*

The car treks uphill, towards the attic. Austin starts screaming, "I can't go on. I can't go back...Father."

The confusion among the voices is more than it was when he first entered the house. Laughter. Noises of people requesting that he be quiet: shhh shhh. The attic is ten feet by seven feet and has a height of six feet. There is wood burning in the fireplace. The room is cluttered with debris and historical artifacts. The fireplace door opens. The house is now completely silent. Austin sees a shadow leaning on the wall but can't make out any accompanying person. The shadow was not there when he first entered. The shadow does not move. Then, a second appears. A third. The room begins to fill with shadows. Austin tries to leave the car. He looks left. Right. Front. He is afraid because the shadows are standing still. All he sees are their blood red eyes. In the past the shadows danced around the room to a sound only they could hear. Perhaps his father could also hear the music. His father used to laugh and clap to it, but he never heard the sound. But these shadows remain still

Austin's heart races. His pores open. He screams to release the fears he once held back.

An invisible force lifts a paper scroll. He hears the keeper's voice. "It is our duty to treasure. Our duty to keep the folds to which we are bound."

Austin interrupts, "We can't live by the past."

The keeper continues, "Who will call the day? Who will free the 'night? To ensure that all can step forward into a new day." Austin does not answer. The shadows laugh. The room starts to rock like a ship about to capsize. The shadows vanish one after the other. The keeper is all that is left. "With all your knowledge. All your losses. Your family. How could you let it go on?"

"I thought you shadows were the enemy."

"How can we, the past, be your enemy?"

Austin's confidence builds, feeling that even the keeper knows that the *House of Fear* is really a tug-of-war between the past and the future. "You live in the middle therefore you are bound."

"Nothing is pure and free in life. Nothing!" She walks up close to the car.

"You are asking me to sacrifice the present in order to live in the past. You want the past to continue forever, as if it is the present, the gift of life."

The keeper claps her hands once then vanishes.

Austin stands and spreads his arms the way the keeper had done on the lawn. The result is not as he expected. He simply falls out of the car. He remains down on the floor, looking up as the shadows reappear. Austin hears the music. It has a ceremonial ring to it. The shadows clap to the sound, one clap at a time.

One says, "Let us close by giving thanks to the union that has created this house."

Another shadow steps forward, snatching a scroll from the air, and reads:

> *Here we have a buck wild African animal. Listed at six feet, four inches. Two hundred and forty-five pounds. He will one day in another hyphenated form enlist to help this country fight in order to prolong the reign. May it rain for this animal. May it pour.*
>
> *Let the bidding start at two cattle and two horses; do we have a counter offer.*

The first shadow approaches and spits on Austin's body.

A third shadow comes forward, grabs a book from the rubble on the floor then begins to read:

*As he lay before us, a lost soul. A being on which conditioning took toll. Let's not forget the cloudy skies in which he flew. The knowledge that he knew...*

Austin rises to his knees, "Are you because you know? Or do you really understand the plight of tomorrow, or the moral of history?"

The third shadow knocks Austin unconscious with a blow to the back of the head then continues,

*...the quest for which he rests. Let all know that in order to pass the test of the best, he jested.*

The keeper steps forward. "I will be his gatherer if thou will keep the frame as if it were the same, like all soldiers who have bent when sent down the river with only an oar and nothing but their souls to spend."

The third shadow, one with the book agrees. The keeper and the shadows leave the room by walking down the stairs. Hours later, Austin awakes, rubbing his eyes to adjust to the room's level of darkness. He hears buzzing around the room. Feels a presence lurking, his heart pounds. The fireplace door opens. A voice asks, *"Who?"*

He does not answer.

"Know you not your own, Austin?"

"Jonathan!!!"

"Not just him, everyone! Your legacy!" An invisible hand

smacks him. He hears gunshots and fights back his screams. His fear has become a living cell. It materializes near his left foot and rises into a shadow.

The horrors of the house force him to question why he has returned. "For the family. For the kids." He walks to the attic's lone window and sees Sarah and Dennis exiting the park, holding Peggy's hands. Brad lingers behind them, and does not look as sad as they do. Austin feels saddened that he never fully explained his history to them, to explain it was such that he could abandon her, her kids and his only son.

Brad turns and looks up at the attic. He shouts, "Of the mind, body and soul. Daddy be bold."

The sound of the keeper's steps on the stairs and her return to the attic does not startle him. She joins him by the window. "I will always be by his side until his time comes. As for the others, they are on their own since this has nothing to do with them. But tonight, let us rejoice. For one of the greats has returned to prove that a man who knows but does not understand is nonetheless a man."

Austin is not willing to celebrate. "Worshipping at the altar of the past is not a victory to me."

"But, it is our legacy, all of ours. And, we worship the past whether we realize it or not."

"A man cannot be judged, a soul cannot be passed unless there is an understanding."

The keeper spreads her arms. "For the reclamation be true. My son, you are. You are." As Austin steps into the living cell turned shadow, the keeper pushes the car out the side of the attic down a chute that leads to the parking lot. Peggy, Sarah and Dennis run and crowd the empty rickety car. Brad ignores it, continuing to walk the empty parking lot toward the lone remaining vehicle.

As he and the keeper vanish, Austin says, "Hopefully the empty car will convince them that I am gone."

The keeper nods, adding, "And, that there are levels of being to which they are not privy, and understandings so unorthodox, they will under no circumstance understand the path."

# Nickel Bag Revolutionaries

"How should I say this?" That is how I started my conversation with Phil about her. "How should I say this without making it sound like I am bragging?" Don't, was his reply. Rebuttal wasn't my weapon, so I let Phil get away with his rude response. I saw through him. It was his attempt to distance himself from my constant self-aggrandizement over my lack of sympathy for Darlene.

We were sitting in my little cube of a room philosophizing our existence the way we used to do two or three times a week. Even though my mother was away visiting her mother and sisters, we did not use the living room. It was our way of showing respect for her understanding ways. The apartment had two small bedrooms and no hallways. It was a square space, spliced up into four equal parts with the bathroom taking a piece of each of the bedrooms. Unlike the neighborhood's brownstones, we had low ceilings and the walls had no details, just flat sheets bought at a local home improvement store. The whole apartment was painted white, now turned dingy from the many years without a new coat of paint. We sat in my room as if it were a war room, a sacred place, like the empty canyons where frontier men exploring new terrain would sit by the campfire, made from a hole they dug with bare hands or crude tools, then filled with twigs and paper. It was a starless, moonless night in the dead of winter, and the urban sounds were in effect. From my little abode, with the windows cracked, we could hear the corner businessmen trash about the tales of future plight.

*You wait. And see the ride I'm going to have come June next year.*

*That girl from down the street said she's going to come by next week.*

It used to amaze me how thin plots turned into such shocking, and grand stories, but now I realize a novel idea does not a novel make.

Take Phil for instance. He used to talk about equality, as if it were a poem. It had color, similarities, and it existed as if it were on par with and within every person, as if the rhythm was built on the foundation that all beings took one step at a time.

We were seated behind bamboo shades. I was on the bed. He sat on a trunk of memorabilia. "Do you ever think of the headless horseman?"

Lacking seriousness, I answered in a carefree manner, as if the wind blowing outside was mine alone. "That was the first native we tried to scalp! Bad job, eh?" Phil didn't see or attempt to build upon the nervy wit. He just sat there then took a puff on the marijuana joint we were sharing. He stared at me for a few minutes then tried to escape my trapped state of slight embarrassment, saying he wanted to get home in time to catch

Carson. He claimed it was a repeat of one that we both saw together and thought it to be one of Johnny's best. It was the show where Johnny goofed on all the actors who, because of their acting fame were allowed to make records. "Oh, that's on again? It has to be the best ever."

Phil smiled then took a sip from the large mug with the red punch. It was my mug but Phil often did things like drink from my mug. It was his way of trying to share whatever hardship or gratifying state I was experiencing. "Would you make a record if you had the chance?"

The words jumped out of my mouth because I was glad that Phil had gotten back into steps for our witty banter. "Hell yeah!"

"What if it didn't do well? What if it ended up costing you more than what you make from it?"

"It's not about cost. It's about opportunity."

Phil chuckled then said in Columbus-like discovery, "You've changed."

Change? What is change? Is it two quarters and five dimes? Or is it one dollar and seven quarters? "That's vague, Phil."

"Come on Tim, you know what I mean."

Tim? Why would Phil call me by that name? As far as I know, he doesn't even know a person named Tim. I was about to ask him

if it were possible for an abstract creation

to be more whole than a creation built as a whole,

but he interrupted me. "How was it really with her?"

Here, we were talking about change, about how a whole gets broken into little pieces, and whether the fractions, the fractured pieces can have more meaning than the original whole. Then, Phil turns around and brings up Darlene.

I didn't respond in hopes that he would find the matter a bit too personal for me to talk of. But he just stared at me, the look, the face of a nine year-old inquiring about the true meaning of not being promoted by the teacher at the end of the school year. His eyes, deep and moist, with the balls situated nearly half an inch behind the bridge of his brow. His lips were parted enough for me to see the string of saliva uniting his top and bottom two front teeth, and for him to whisper, "I thought we were friends. I thought we could share those kinds of moments."

I thought we were friends too. In fact: we were. It's just that each friend serves a different function. When one friend shares too much of yourself with you, he or she comes to resemble an enemy. And, as I felt at that moment with Phil, and still feel: Semblance, mind-sight, is more than half, but no more than two-thirds of reality.

Phil was not the friend I wanted to share moments of Darlene with, but if I did not tell him of Darlene, he would no longer be a friend. He would become another enemy masquerading as a friend.

I did not want Phil to haunt me. I didn't.

My uneasiness caused me to fidget, my legs trembling and shifting, accidentally stepping on the side of the ashtray. The ashes spilled on the floor. Phil was about to pick them up, but I asked him to leave them.

"My grandmother once told me that it is bad luck to spill ashes and not make a valid effort to replace them in their natural place."

He had that genuinely worried look on his face. The last time I saw that look was when I lied and told him that mall security had apprehended me and taken my ID for boosting gear.

Then he tried again to pick up the ashes.

I quickly stepped off the bed and took hold of him, grabbing both wrists. Questioningly, he looked at me. As our eyes converged like perpendicular lines, I knew what his unstated words would be. I knew that although the television commercial was playing a jingle of new and improved, for some detergent that claimed to wash away the dirt, we had digressed from plotters of the next generation's trends and goals to modern day singers of the theme of parity.

I should have simply told Phil to go and find out for himself, but I did not want to end our friendship on a sour note. So, I tried to search for a new starting point. I broke the contact. The way I let go of his wrists indicated that he was free to do as he pleased. He chose to leave the ashes on the floor. As I rested back on the sand-colored bedspread, I stared at the ceiling, for the first time noticing the agonic nature of the lines created from my upstairs neighbor's leaky pipe.

I waited for Phil to break the silence and set in motion the wheels of his faint and undeserving quest for knowledge of my time with Darlene, but he did not say anything. It wasn't as if he was at a loss for words—no, not, never Phil. He was waiting for me to begin so he could, when confronted by me as to why he told others, state that I offered it freely, as if it were not truly personal, as if it were not the truth.

"You're smooth," I said then stood on the bed to touch the lines on the ceiling, feeling their dampness, wondering how come the water never leaked through. Then I sat back down. With my fingers locked within each other, arms extended and parallel to my buckling knees and feet lightly planted on the floor, I began telling him the tales of incongruous labor. Of how Darlene got on top and rode me, and I had the pleasure of just lying there. Phil sat and absorbed it. Never saying stop, enough or pause. Not even when I wept in blank verse.

He just soaked each word in like the sponge I once hoped he would never become. Ooohing and aaahing like a true spectator while I made a spectacle of myself.

What spectacle? We were friends.

Were we still friends after he let me

tell him how

I once laughed at

the deformity of her left

breast which caused

her right nipple to

swell three times

its normal size? Were we?

If we were, I could have let it slide. I could have let his pleasant, absorbing gawk symbolize the result of a young man's curiosity being filled to capacity. But we were not.

In his nonchalant yet bedlam-like way of corresponding, I could see him worming his way to parity, as if he had been there with me. His crawling under my skin, his bony fingers clinging onto my neck and his mouth shut, not sharing a part of his state.

Eleven o'clock came so Phil decided to go home. He got up and grabbed his sweatshirt and coat. His movements, haggard and out of sync, the way one rises in the morning in a dark room searching for the alarm clock, positioned across the room to ensure the sleeper does not simply roll over and slam the alarm off. The way he dressed, the speed, the pattern of sweatshirt, ski hat, gloves then coat told me he had a secret, perhaps another bit of wisdom he was trying not to share.

I have known Phil since second grade. Ours was an acquaintance fortified by a rap song's hook that "life as a shorty shouldn't be so rough." We wore tattered rags, got to school early for breakfast and ate lunch in the cafeteria using the tickets handed out to the poor children. Through nearly a decade we helped each other by passing the wisdom of how to survive and, perhaps, one day thrive in life.

As sixth graders we started smoking weed to avoid becoming drug pushers. The local dealers were an organized, disciplined army. You either sold for them or bought from them. Our plight was similar to small underdeveloped countries, used as funnels so larger countries could amass wealth.

The first time neighborhood youths approached us we didn't have any money. Their words and manner were calm, but the message was clear. The next day, Phil came to school with money. For the next two years, Phil either came with money or drugs. Whenever I asked about the money, he said his grandmother gave it to him. Whenever I asked about the drugs, he said he bought the drugs with the money that his grandmother gave him. I never really believed him but I had no other explanation.

The summer before high school, Phil said his grandmother could no longer give him money, so we got our first jobs, off the books. Each season, I would switch jobs to fit my school schedule. Phil never stayed at one job too long and, at times, went months without a job. But, he always had money or drugs. After we got high, we would eat.

I guess that's why I overreacted to Phil's response when I said, "I could definitely use one of Big Tone's BBQ late night specials."

"My grandmother always said not to eat spicy food late 'cause..."

"Oh, fuck your grandmother!" He wasn't upset by my remark. He simply gave a dumb–*you are my best buddy and only my best buddy can say things like that to me*–chuckle and kept walking by my side. I too laughed. At first it was a burst then it turned into a hysterical convulsion, the type reserved for lunatics who've been proclaimed as such.

As if he were on par, Phil said, "You shouldn't do that." I ignored his warning as one of his many calculated entrances into the inner-workings of my mind. "My grandmother died in a mental hospital a week after a laugh like that. She began hallucinating, complaining of seeing images and linking random happenings, trying to make them into one linear event."

We arrived in front of the late night food stand, and he said that he would see me tomorrow. I said likewise. As he began his slow ascension to the subway's elevated platform he turned and said, "On her deathbed, Grandma said it had to do with getting it off her chest. But to the rest of us, she simply lost her head."

I nodded then turned into the store. Leaving with my order of a roasted half-chicken meal, I began picking on the meat while walking the four blocks to my apartment. A car traveling eastward honked and the man in the shotgun seat waved at me. I didn't get a chance to see who it was, so I just returned the gesture, with the satisfaction that he knew me.

The gloomy looking tree in front of the bodega dropped a few leaves. As I passed, I turned, expecting to see someone behind me, but there was no one there. Upon turning back around, I was in my room. I wondered where the ashes went. At first, I thought my mom must have come in and picked them up. That was not possible because she was not due back for at least five more days.

I heard something move underneath the bed, rustling like mice in between wall panels. My first impulse was to run out of the apartment, but instead I looked to see what it was. What I saw had no true form. The best way to describe it was that of an enlarged gelatin version of a man. It clutched the bottom of my box spring, curled up in the fetal position. It pretended, for a minute or so, not to see me then it spoke. "So you've finally decided to open up?"

"What?" The fact that it spoke English eased my fear and concern.

"All these years have gone by. We've been waiting. How old are you now?"

At first, I did not answer because I was insulted that this

wanna-be scary figure wanted to engage me. To find out why it was here, I decided to answer. "Seventeen." About to ask a question of my own, I nearly choked on a small chicken bone. I was a bit shaken because I had never been one to daydream or drift off especially while walking the harsh pavements of the reality.

I reached the corner nearest to my home and sparked

a dull conversation with the two

youths, businessmen, who were and are still

in their own way surviving

by the only means afforded to them.

"What's up! Let me get another nickel bag."

The younger one, no more than fourteen, sized me up. "What's this your third for the day? You alone gonna pay for my new ride."

I nodded, glancing at the other one. We were in grade school together. The last time I saw him attending school for actual education was the seventh grade. Since then, I have seen him lurking the hallways like a ghoul haunts a mansion, a mere shadow ducking the school's security guards, often holding court in bathroom stalls where he conducts his business. The older soldier nodded back as if confirming my suspicion that this new recruit was a mere sacrificial lamb, either for the police or the rival drug gang.

We slapped five like teammates congratulating a score; he slipped me the weed and I gave him the money. As I strolled away, I noticed the city had yet to replace the streetlight's bulb of the pole that illuminated the corner up to the middle of the block where my building stood. So, the block was dark. With each tree passed, the sounds of leavings moving with the night breeze enhanced the senses. It was easy to mistaken the urban sounds and think that one was being followed.

I opened the lobby door and heard screams. The noise seemed to have come from upstairs, on the opposite end of the hall, where I lived. I was about to run to see if anything was wrong but dismissed the screams as objects of my imagination. As soon as I removed the key from the door's lock, a masked figure accosted me and pinned me against the door.

We were in the vestibule. It had its hands around my neck, choking as if to say it wanted more than my death. More than death? At that time, I could not fathom such a thing.

The figure was not a masculine presence, not for the lack of strength, but for the method that it used to drag me. My body was fully stretched out, with my knees hitting the edge of every step, and the pain rippling throughout my body. My eyes shut on their own, as if reassuring me that sight was unnecessary because I had no control of my destination; my breath was somewhat stifled, struggling with each exhale. The masked figure stated that it would let me choose my own fate.

We arrived at my apartment and before I had a chance to ask how we were able to filter through the door, it dragged me into my room. The figure walked into the television, dragging me along onto a production set.

I had always watched the box but had never been in it or on it.

I got up and started dancing to show that I was willing to do anything. Then she said, "Sing! Sing!"

*Each day through my window*
*I watch her as she passes by*
As I got to the chorus of the first song that came to mind
*but it was just my imagination*
*once again*
*Running away with me.*

The figure screamed, "Shut up, damn it!"

She pushed me out of the tube and onto my twin-size bed. The robe only allowed me to see three cavities. Her eyes were tear-filled and she was tight-lipped. I removed the clothes off my back because I was sweating from the excitement, and with anticipation of what could come next. I kneeled on the mattress and asked, "What's wrong?"

She sang, "Jealousy. Envy. Hate."

"Exactly!" I shouted then tried to stick my hands through the television to pull her out. The futile effort left me with a rapidly pounding heart and hoarse larynx with which I kept repeating "Darlene" until I caught myself in the lobby with the door still open.

I closed the lobby door and ran upstairs to my second floor apartment. The only thing on my mind was to go to my room, afraid that they would not be there, but the ashes were exactly where I had spilled them. Realizing how I had compromised Darlene and myself just to remain friends with Phil scared me. I knelt to pick up the ashes and placed them in the ashtray.

Comfort was for a brief moment my niche. I undressed, except for my briefs and got in bed. I was trembling with fear, and then it materialized from the ashtray. The ashes floated up, each connecting to the next, forming a frightening figure. It inhaled as if gaining the breath of life. It wore a black robe, resembling that of a monk's living in a monastery.

From the sides of the hood, I could tell that it had ashen gray hair, scaly skin and barren eyes. It began to feel as if she were becoming part of me, her body, an extension of my limbs, saddling me as if I was her property. She was not heavy on my body, but she was truly overtaking my mind.

"What are you in it for?" I asked.

"The ride. Just for the ride."

"What if it leads to nowhere?"

She turned and grinned. "It will. It will, if only you let me steer."

Days have gone by, perhaps even years, but it doesn't seem so. Phil and some other folks came to visit, but only once since that night. I don't recall talking to them because I was lying down, somewhat asleep. They have not returned since that day. When and if someone else returns, then I will conclude that it's the next day and life has changed.

I have not left my room or the sight of the ashes since that night. I sneak a peek at the outside world by peeping out of the sides of my bamboo shades. I saw snow this morning and felt humidity and haziness this afternoon. Everyday looks and feels different. But, unlike the past, the changes seem erratic. The temperature goes from hot to cold in a very random pattern.

I sometimes look for hours at the tray of my ashes, wondering about the headless horseman, how he lost his head. Each time I plan to go out, my ashes drag me by force, back to bed, with a simple thought, why bother to experience the danger of life if it is able to take you without cost?

It is mind-sight, a form of blindness that guides me through this darkness, helping me to recall the glory of my past, like a promise that the glory will soon return. There once was a fire in the building next door. The fire trucks came but the building still burned down to the ground. My guide told me not to worry, that it was not my time to go. And, that if one whom I've seen before comes again to visit, then it is my time to go. But since neither has happened, I will sit here and let my ashes run away with me.

# Dime Store Divas

Dime Store Divas is a period piece. It is an ending. To some, it is a mere pause. In actuality it is a complete stop. Even if father returns home, it will not be the continuation of a former life filled with promise and spent in compromise.

That's how Louis put it, where he placed the blame.

You knew there were some moments when the marriage was just that, failed promises and compromise. But you saw them as the price for happiness, meals at five-star restaurants, monthly getaways, and designer clothes when there is no sale. You inadvertently taught Faye, a father was just that, a little girl's ability to make a fashion statement.

Faye had become his favorite girl. At five, with large whites and small pupils, she had become your spitting image. Had learned the power of a smile and a whine. Knew to sit on daddy's lap, throw both arms around his neck and plant a big kiss on his cheek, then say thank you. You and Faye thought he lived for the adulation. But, the monthlies threw him for a loop. The payment cycle cut him so deep, the bills were bleeding him dry. So, he said.

During the finger-pointing episode, you defended yourself by stating that you spent the money on Faye and the upkeep of the household. His income carried the load. Then, without your knowledge he did the math, and on Faye's ninth birthday, he asked that you return to the workforce. For you, that was the end. The courtship was based on his climbing the ladder, and you raising the family. His argument that one child is not a family was his choice. You wanted at least three children, but Louis said to wait until you two were in a better financial situation.

As if he knew your train of thought, he started using condoms the day you secretly got off the pill. To spite him and try to force a compromise, you refused to work and tried to make his life harder by not maintaining the household. His petition for a divorce left only one question. What about Faye? He said not to worry. Not to involve the judicial system. The two lawyers worked out an agreement. He would still pay the full upkeep of the house and an additional ten percent of his monthly gross for Faye's personal things. All you had to do was get a basic gig, perhaps part-time. Instead, you chose to poison her mind. Painted a picture to her and your friends of an irresponsible father who left as his daughter was crying.

Said that his not giving enough money was the reason Faye had to start shopping at low-budget stores, penny pinching at the five and dime. She never got his side of the story because she never asked, and he never told anything against you. In her mind, it was a matter of time before she would get her working papers for after-school and summer employment. When she spoke of work, Louis saw it as her having adopted his values. She only wanted to do it to afford nicer clothes, but he never really noticed the quality difference in her clothes. To him, her diction and behavior was how he measured her childhood development.

Summer youth employment, at a local college during the summer before senior year in high school, opened her eyes to an independent woman's mindset and power. She loved to hear them talk about payday and their plans for their next purchase or trip. All of them had degrees and counseled her to further her education. By the time Faye left for college, she had stopped the visits by either blowing him off when he called or not showing up after confirming. Still, he sent her gifts and extra spending money. You had succeeded in isolating him but could not tell that she was only tolerating you until she could be out on her own.

College was ready for Faye. Swallowed her up like dishwater going down the drain. Though she managed not to gain the freshman fifteen, she thought she had weight. Tossed her hair off her shoulders, smiled and partied hard. Learned to hold her liquor, pull deep on the zigzag smoke and keep her composure after standing on lines. To her credit, the drugs weren't why she hung on the scene as if auditioning to become a starlet. The men were her vice. Had become such since Bye-Bye Lenny pinned her against the wall at a high school basement party and slid his right ring finger through the side of her pink panties. At thirteen, fresh meat in high school, she started dating him, a leader in the circle of ringers, smalltime hustler who never veered more than six miles away from his birthplace, yet had the nerve to have a nationwide plan for his cellie and a two-way pager, yet had no internet connection or email address.

As in high school, Faye knew the power and vulnerability of being a pretty young thing. Though she partied and kept the façade of fast girl no rules, she kept her lovers to a minimum and took the pill on a regular. Yet she had to admit that college life was different. Living away on one's own. How the major players had little money and no hustle, yet shot their game straight with no chaser. She knew the deal when she indirectly agreed to become Kappa Kenny's Wednesday night, left scrotum girl, swallower of depleted nuts. Leftovers. It took Faye a whole year to realize that the college week began on Thursday night. Get your party and freak on until Sunday dusk. Then hit the books until Thursday dusk. So Wednesday night was when major players rested and released excess energy.

By the end of the first year and his graduation, to which she was not invited as a special guest, she felt that she had maintained her dignity and image because she was not the "do his homework" girl. Faye and Dime Store Divas, in general, know how to focus on the top layer of things. To her all that mattered was that he was graduating with honors, was cheating on his "real" girlfriend and not her, wore a fraternity brand on his left pect and had a good job waiting for him.

During the summer, she felt as if she had graduated. You never asked when she'd be home. She did the party circuit and knew she had to move on to bigger things such as KAOS, as in Kappa Alpha Omega Sigma parties, boat rides and anything she could afford. While living the college luxurious life, she gained an interest in DAZS, as in the Deltas, AKAs, Zetas and Sigmas.

Studied them hard to see which was more her style and who would accept her. So the first semester of her sophomore year, Faye wore her hair in a bun, kept her name out of the grapevine and limited her partying to only the top campus events. One thing she forgot though: higher achievement in college was predicated on the books. By the third semester, she had done two straight semesters on academic probation after barely getting a 2.1 on a 4.0 point scale in her very first semester.

Faye disappeared without a clue, like spring in global warming times. Since she was a loner, no one knew the real story. Word she help spread was that school up there had gotten lame, and she needed to be in the big city, doing big things. Got a job as a sec'y who roved as a receptionist during lunch hours. Could no longer stand living with you, so she got an apartment of her own.

Her roommate, Loose Booty Judy, her girl since tenth grade. That didn't last long. Judy was living another form of Dime Store Divahood. She was a criminal-minded booster and major scammer. A topless dancer, who when she needed the extra loot, brought club customers to the rest. Judy would hit them off for the right price. She was also a switch-hitter, and as if baiting Faye, walked around the apartment in her thong. Messy broad, always sloppy drunk or high, quick to cuss a person out and thought Faye was living slow and basically a nerd. Tried to beat Faye out of two months rent.

They got into a scuffle, catfight— scratches from acrylics, pulled weaves and torn t-shirts. Faye moved out. A few months later, they accidentally bumped into each other at an upscale department's store half-off sale and they made the peace. Not to the point where Faye gave her the number to her new spot, a tiny basement joint in somebody's one-family home. Live and learn was how Faye rationalized the situation with her former roommate. The four months living with Judy convinced her that she needed to get back in school, even if she had to attend at night.

Clap for her, for she managed to do undergrad in six and a half years while maintaining a full-time job, switching workplaces now and then, and climbing up the ladder. Now that school was done and she had a lighter schedule, Faye began to live her dream of vacationing at the hotspots like she did when she was a little girl.

Armed with a degree, she regained some of her lost confidence, started considering herself a scholar. Started hanging out on the bourgie, beige people wearing khaki with loafers set. Plus, she was clubbing at thirty years old, had a gym membership to keep it tight, and kept appointments to get her hair done every weekend.

Shortly after her thirtieth birthday, I remember meeting her at a Nupe jam. She said Dude was too short though she was only five-five. Still Dude kept her talking, made her smile and laugh, all night. Faye agreed to give me her number because the release, laughter, had been missing in her life. That night as we parted, everything about her, especially her look and conversation, told me she was an oversexed surface dweller, a shallow broad who used dates, the courtship ritual, as a meal ticket, and boyfriends as plane tickets and cardboard figures for special occasions where pictures would be taken. When we hooked up for lunch on the following Wednesday, Faye acted as if she was the one hiring. She didn't realize that it was mid-May and Dude was looking for a replacement killer, a scab for seasonal, no chance of promotion employment.

I still didn't get why, after the hard road she had walked, she was maintaining the same old diva attitude of returning food such as rice, harassing waitresses like she was at the local Red Lobster. She then tried to play that intellectual, where did you go, grow up, wanna be in five years! Oh, the State U. My last boyfriend went to Morehouse, this and that...I flipped the script and put her on the defensive by asking where she went, her age and whether she was too old to be doing the boyfriend bit. What made Faye tolerable was that Dude had met a whole lot of Dime Store Divas who had no dinero, talking the same old, father left, times got rough, don't trust no man. I told her not to sweat the past and that the U.S. is still kool with England, France and Spain.

Though Faye's face drew a blank at that analogy, she was a good actress and pretended to get what I was saying. Faye had a high tolerance until Dude asked her why she keeps Dude around. That was the last time she came by, called– even on the return, and had sex with me.

Faye was full of assumptions on what Dude should do to be with her. She thought the rap she used where she pretended to be a fag hag would work on me. But I had seen better-equipped women run that same game and turn horny men into platonic boyfriends, shoulders to cry on, ears to blow smoke in.

Up to the fourth time that we hooked up for either lunch or drinks, things were kool and platonic. She had begun to confide in me as if Dude wasn't a hetero, and was not willing to spend on material that Dude can get for free. She drew me a road map to her weaknesses and her soft spot. As I pulled the car in front of her apartment to drop her off, she hugged me like I was her father, complete with the kiss on the cheek. All I could do was laugh. I am not sure if Dude's laugh confused her, but she wanted to know what was so funny. I chuckled and rubbed my belt buckle. She laughed at Dude, stating that it would never work. I closed the deal by telling her to let me know when she got tired. Nine and a half weeks later, she told me that she could no longer take it, that she could not breathe and needed her space. Girl had never even been to Dude's apartment, and she was falling in love.

Then and now, a Dime Store Diva holds no regrets. Even if she did, she would not wear it around her neck like a gaudy medallion, or shade her eyes with designer wear. Faye bore her scars as if the crest of a secret society; to the public like sagging breasts in a plunging neckline; for she has come to accept them as the scars of her tribe.

That night at the club, we made a conscious effort not to approach each other. Our only sign of recognition: half a head nod and half a smile. Near closing time, at four a.m., she was still there, flittering between the pool table in the lounge area where the poseurs, in crowded thousand-people nightclubs, hang out. She was sipping some nouveau martini, her eyes looking up at some guy's Adam's Apple.

II

Not just some guy. A tough guy. Starvin Marvin was what they called him when he was a kid. He owned only four pairs of pants and wore them in an offbeat cycle for the school year. Would always find a reason to be at the next man's around dinnertime. His story was well-documented in the media and it was similar to Faye's. He was another form of Dime Store Diva.

Raised by mother because as a father, you were–*a shot glass in one hand, hat tilted to the side, hanging at the local watering hole, hollering at some twenty-six year-old chick*–type of guy. That's how Marvin's mom met you. You were both poor people and hooked up strictly because life had limitations and its core truth was that the game was meant to be played. So you played doctor then house. Times were rough but manageable until you got tired of playing husband and daddy. Cicely could have handled you not playing one role, but not both. So thirteen years and four kids later, Cicely got friends asking her, "Girlfriend, how could you let him treat you so bad?" All they ever saw was your trifling ways. All she ever heard were the rumors. Cicely had come to yearn for only a new truth, and that was for you to help pay the damn bills.

To you, this marriage had one refrain, time and its practical applications. Cicely didn't understand why you wasted so much time hanging out with your friends. You didn't understand why she let time do her figure and her mind so bad, to the point she thought you were no good. You thought she was acting out, acting old, nagging the man out of his house and down the road, way past yonder...a warp signature...caught in the annals of time where twenty-six was the cut-off age for a woman to be considered a dime. By then a woman should either be married or have at least one child to prove that she was reasonable enough for some man to have left his seed. You told Cicely that at thirty-nine, she was not to expect some next man to come and take care of her and the kids.

At seven, Marvin became the man of the house. Third child but first boy. Cicely was raised on old school ways and made due by getting a part-time job to go with her regular job. She believed daughters are girls forever but should be treated as women as soon as they are able to wash their own stuff. From there, give them the added responsibility of laundry, cleaning and fixing the household's meals. Though the title of man has been affixed on their chest, sons should be treated as boys until they are able to take care of their mothers.

So Cicely kept an eye on Marvin. Put the word out to the neighborhood women that she be notified if anyone caught Marvin slipping. It was a woman thing, a secret society whose primary objective was to protect the boys so they'll one day be there for their mamas.

Meanwhile, first daughter, Shirley got her curves then swerved off the path of chores around the house, and right into cheapie around the way. It was a glorious moment from a picturesque, artistic standpoint–the way she let time smack her with two toddlers before high school's end, and right into Aid to Families with Dependent Children. Happened so fast that Cicely was actually proud of her daughter. Made space for her at the crib.

For Cicely had seen teen pregnancy in hers and other families throughout her life.

Nearly fourteen, second daughter, Bridget was flying through her teenage years. Had an image problem since five years old, so she used petroleum jelly, to soften the darkness. Instead it made her glow, and caused the kids to call her Greasy. She hated the nickname and fought and cussed the kids but Greasy stuck anyway. Eventually she took to the nickname because it made her stand apart. That, and her gift of gab that she used to jab at other people's insecurities and misfortunes, gained her popularity. In her clique, she diverted attention. First, as cheap wine drinker and occasional dime bag buyer, she boosted clothes and sold them cheap on the streets. Then, as a mad crack smoker, Greasy Bridget sold herself cheap on the streets.

As a high school senior, Marvin was All-City, Three-Letter Man. Passed on Football because he was a quarterback being asked to convert. Wide Receiver scared him because too many of the neighborhood boys had gone to jail. Since Track and Field rarely came on TV, he ran away from it. In those days, Marvin was playing sports only for the dream of making lots of money and achieving national fame. And, for his family. So he used his cross-over, hand-eye coordination and decent grades as leverage. Never outright said it, but the college recruiters knew there would have to be money under the table. So they got the point they wanted.

The Midwest was stormy but as long as things were calm at home, Marvin directed the offense and hid behind his toughness. Being tough for a man has more to do with growing a thick skin than it does bench pressing.

Looking at Marvin, you never see his real eyes. What you see is a shield, hiding the years and tears of receiving a call that his little brother, Brandon, got smoked over territory. Fifteen years-old. Was a mama's boy until thirteen. Got respect because Marvin went from starvin to carvin turkeys at all kinds of tables. But, Brandon wanted his own rep. There came the need for a new family. The Glock Assembly, gun toters and drug hustlers. High school vandals. The bathroom was their storefront. The cafeteria, their stage, the war room that turned the streets into a battleground.

Brandon's obituary might as well have been written in Braille because his crew carried on as if they could not see their deaths coming. Eulogized by Shirley who now had a third child. Marvin's broad shoulders helped carry the coffin. Appalled that his family was squandering this opportunity of financial stability, he demanded that they get their act together. That was his first taste of his father's medicine.

Women don't listen to men, even if the funds are flowing. Why should they when the lineage is handed down through them? To them what men say is not the whole truth. For a man's story is only written on his back. Women have their stories written on their backs, as well as their guts because big-headed Marvin and the likes of him could not pass through. So women have either broken pelvises that time never truly healed, and the scars of having their guts cut open. C-Section-8 – for clarity in the duality.

So Marvin headed back to the Midwest. The deal he made to

have the invisible money reach the family was that he would stay four years. But national recognition is a temptress, a short voluptuous woman that gives only a small window of opportunity. So, during his junior year, averaging a double-double and a half at a top-ranked program, he was ready to face the consequences of reneging on his promise. The coach knew it. So, in anticipation, Coach S recruited a point guard. During the final half of the season, Marvin learned that fast break also has a dual meaning.

It led to a rough rehab period for a reconstructed knee. Though the dream would not be deferred, Marvin leaned back on the smile of Serenity Smith. She, a local girl working her way through college, was majoring in Physical Rehabilitation. This was her internship year. Preparing to attend medical school. To one day open her own practice. Got a chance to practice her skill as a counselor. Not only did she help Marvin find peace with his injury, he realized that he was actually in school and learned to use his education as a crutch. Switched from Basket Weaving as a major to Finance. Got a job in the big city at an investment firm for the summer, back East, near home, but far enough from his family.

In the fall, he followed the course the doctor and Serenity laid out for him. He would study as hard as he would play, coming off the bench because Coach S had promised the freshman, high school All-American that he would start. It was the same promise he had made to Marvin during recruitment. So, Marvin worked on his jump shot, hoping to get some minutes at the shooting guard position along with the point. The night before the first home game, in the openness of the campus' largest quad, as the sky grayed and the moon wore the sky like a mask, as if the finished canvas of an impressionist painting, Marvin and Serenity made love for the first time. They had had sex before but had never fully undressed their emotions. She was wearing a short skirt with no panties and he had his pants and draws around his knees. As she rocked back and forth on his lap, he said them then she repeated the three words, I love you. Not just Love Ya, as he often said to his family.

The words stayed with them until the next fall when Serenity Smith realized that like men, seasons did not change, they left. Yes, they came back but if you knew what to look for, you would realize that it was not the same season. For time had marched on, and time marchers did the same.

Marvin was not drafted. Got invited to two NBA training camps. Chose one. Did not make the team. Planned to play overseas. Serenity got into Meherry. Turned down his engagement. She realized that he, after all, loved the game. It was either that or he craved the fame and money so much that first love was a hindrance. Middle class status, failure. The game, however, was perpetual. Marvin made the pros after years of toiling overseas. Was having a good year then the second knee gave. He rehabbed again but never regained top form. Was doing the CBA thing. Earning a ten-day contract here and there. Enjoying his last days as a professional athlete. Had decided to retire after this season, at age thirty-one, and put his education and those various spurts of employment to use. Top on his list was broadcast journalism or becoming a sports agent.

At first he was living the luxurious life off of what he had saved and was basically doing the club thing. What got Dude was how Marvin and Faye hooked up. As they compared stories around the pool table, they seemed to be licking then bandaging one another's wounds. The fact that they had confined their lives to the surface did not bother them. Unlike when Dude and Faye talked, Marvin saw the symmetry not the inequality. They saw the worth of each other's struggle.

Their union showed me that Dime Store Divas is a period piece. Of a ladder with a missing rung. A masterpiece capturing those whose legacy is tainted by deft, razor-like strokes, etched in an unfixed pattern across a human's back. To achieve their former royal status, Dime Store Divas stretch themselves across life's canvas and allow their struggle to be painted as an original, ugly picture. The truth is twisted, two-sided and two-faced. Dime Store Divas is a period piece meaning the end to two families' struggle, a return to what home was meant to be. Or is it the dead-end of marriage, over-consumption and no community involvement? Is it divorcing yourself from the community, not reaching your hand back to help pull others up so they do not fall in between the crack, the missing rung?

# Vanity's Fare

One's not supposed to get caught up in these things.

Interfering in other people's lives, whether they are friends or enemies, is a good way to be seen as an enemy. "Entwined within our genome is a strand for meddling; once loose, this strand becomes our very fiber," so says Sarah. We were sitting at Touffé's on December twentieth, enjoying a large cup of tea sweetened with honey and a drop or two of nineteenth century brandy when Sarah suggested Martha for Frank.

Our initial laughter was brief but not undeserved. When we recovered, we plotted their first meeting.

I arrived with Frank on my right at the peak of Nostalgia Night, the first Tuesday of January. It is the night when all the college students who were home for the holiday season met at Touffé's. Touffé's was Dire County's version of a city's trendy café. Outside, a dozen tables stood with two or three wooden, well-shellacked chairs hovering over them. The back of the chairs were angular, leaning forward a bit, causing their occupants to look hungrier than they really were, like mongooses over recently killed reptiles. During the winter, a fiberglass casing covered the café's outdoor section. When snow fell, the casing gave the place the look of an enclave, encased in a glass bowl, much like the ornaments that adorned living room coffee tables. I remember how I use to shake the glass bowl, to see the snowfall, mixing until it and the water became one. No matter how much I shook, the cabin stood strong, as if proving that the home is the only solid state in an unsteady world. Yet there are some who believe home is replaceable, expandable as one progresses through life. They never realize every home could be cultivated, developed to reflect a person's changing needs. And, that home can always be home.

Frank was a bit uneasy about meeting Martha and did not attempt to hide his discomfort. He repeatedly asked about his looks, attire and her. I reassured him of her pleasant personality and her beauty.

We entered the café and saw her seated with her back to the entrance. She wore a black ribbon around the braid, hanging an inch past her upright shoulders. From under Touffé's stained glass lamps, her skin seemed smooth and fragile, like fine china. Her crème, woolen sweater, with its black buttons lining the back, completed her conservative look.

As we made our way through the café, we stopped at practically every table to exchange greetings with the many who had gone to universities and colleges away from home. Nearly everyone from our graduating class and the most recent one was present for Nostalgia Night. They all appeared more mature. Since we did not stay long enough to chat, I could not tell whether the maturity was just a façade to lay girls or guys they hadn't been able to impress when they were in high school.

Sarah hugged us both, then introduced Frank to Matha.

Martha gave him a warm smile, and he, in return, shook her hand. The handshake seemed a bit too formal, like that of two executives about to sit and discuss business. I hugged Martha. We all made small talk while we waited for the waiter to come and take our order. I wasn't really paying attention to the conversation, only filling in the requisite nods and words whenever necessary, until Frank said, "This place has changed."

In my eyes, Touffé hadn't changed a bit. Perhaps it was because Sarah and I came once or twice every week. Frequenting Touffé had been part of my life since our junior year in high school. Most folks have been coming here since they turned sixteen. It was a ritual, especially Nostalgia Night. This is the place where young and old come to mingle, and where those who had moved away know they can always find a recognizable face. But for others, such as Martha, tonight was the very first time.

Her mother moved here from Maine last year, during my second semester in North Braddock Community College. She was then a senior at Dire County High. When she graduated, she wisely decided to attend college in this town. Lately, very few from our town make such a choice, but those who do go to school here, do so for the same reason. Dire County is home, or their new home. Martha immersed herself into our history, as if all that she had lived lacked perspective. Here, she learned to look at all levels, the surface, above and beneath it. Even words like rich, luxury, poor and enough had their levels.

Frank had never met Martha because she spent last summer away, visiting her father. As we drove to Martha's home, I wanted to go by the lake the way we did during our high school years, after victorious football games, and run across the frozen pond. Both Sarah and Frank said they were not in the mood. I wasn't exactly up for it either, but I felt that after so many of Frank's dull conversations about fun and uplifting life on a larger campus in some foreign place, Martha needed more.

The whole evening she hardly spoke. It was as if she had taken a back seat to Frank's mouth, which after each sentence sounded more and more like an idled racecar revving its engine. All we did was nod. In between nods, I observed the women's eyes, with their focus on Frank's lips, how they moved up and down, with only one discernible rhythm, similar to a windup doll. I could take but so much, so my eyes wandered to Martha's square brow, her flat cheeks and the sheer symmetry of her face. I managed to slip in a few sentences about her beauty. Something Frank hadn't done.

The small talk enabled them to hit it off pretty well but, to my surprise and chagrin, at night's end, he just shook hands with her when I drove her home.

Normally a chatterbox filled with wit and mischievous thoughts, Sarah was unusually quiet. She got that way right before her monthly, but it was not due for at least another eleven days. She wanted to go home but offered no true explanation.

I drove to Frank's home last. The goal was to talk to him like we used to throughout our childhood and see how he was really doing. During Nostalgia Night, the stuff he told dealt with academics, and how challenging he found the work. He never told how the people treated him. Instead of focusing on my words about his well-being, he used guilt to try and convince me, then asked why I never visited him. He said his offer to aid me in transferring and applying to his school still stood. I politely listened without heeding to his self-righteousness. As he left that night, I asked that we get together before he returned to school. An awkward moment passed, then, he agreed.

Two weeks later when we got together, he made a point to mention that we were not to go to Touffé's. Since he was driving, I didn't object much as he took us an hour away into the neighboring county's largest disco. The key attraction seemed to be the presence of strangers, people whom I had no interest of ever knowing. Dire's disco was better and had better-looking women. On the way home, Frank gloated about having a good time and the three women who had agreed to exchange numbers with him. I agreed to having had a good time because best friends understood those kinds of things. And, that's why I tried to hook him up with Martha.

Frank did not return for the summer. He used some internship in Boston as his excuse. Though he never outright said it, Frank had become enamored with everything that didn't include Dire. He had no reason to dislike Dire, but it was clear other places were better fits for his aspirations. He would often send postcards of Boston's top landmarks, with the same last sentence, "Try to come for a visit." I almost went with his parents who visited only because Frank planned to head straight to school instead of coming home for the two weeks before class started. Fearing that they would not see him until Thanksgiving, they made the drive.

Not having Frank around for the summer was particularly hard on Sarah. She had gotten used to my having Frank to pal around with because it left her enough time to just wander when I wasn't around. The more time I spent with her, the more we seemed to drift apart. I suggested that she call Martha, but she said Martha was a homebody. So without any hint that there was friction between us, she accused, "What? You think by putting me together with Martha, you can further control me?"

Since she couldn't explain why she felt such was true, she dropped the matter. Yet, the very next day, she ended an intimate relationship that begun with a courtship during a song with the words, "some things never change." I did not want to let go, for I knew once I did she would eventually leave Dire.

Though I had seen Sarah each day during the summer, I never actually saw the changes that were taking place. I used to know her words and next step by simply looking at her, the narrow eyes with the black irises, the slender neck with that thick vein on the left nape and the wide hips serving anchor to a thin waist. Sarah had never been an impulsive person. Her restlessness started the week after Nostalgia Night, when Frank kept encouraging us to live life on a bigger campus, or "any place besides here."

Sarah decided to follow his advice. The next year, Nostalgia Night brought us to the point where all we could do was share a warm embrace at the train terminal. The kiss and hold gave me hope that when she returned during one of the recesses that I would be able to get her back. From there and once she graduated from school, she would return home.

But she never returned. Had no reason to come back after her parents moved away. They left less than a month after Sarah. Sold their home with no problem. Leaving Dire people forget how many want to live here. The minute a home becomes available, no matter the asking price, people flock to it. That alone should have given Sarah's parents a reason to pause, to perhaps ask those buyers why they were coming. In its simplicity, some only saw a mundane life, thinking the remembrance and celebration of tradition was hokey and corny. Yet, others knew it to be the root of Dire's attraction.

The winter Sarah left, Frank went to visit Martha at my urging. When I suggested it, he rolled his eyes, acting as if he had never thought of her during the past year and that I was forcing him. The next day he told me it was the warmest, most comfortable place he'd ever been. Lucky man! That could have been me. His only complaint was her lack of aggression.

Though he saw her everyday during that winter and the summer after graduation, he never made her his steady. Whenever I saw her and engaged her in small talk, she never expressed any bitterness toward Frank. She even went to his wedding.

Two years passed, and postcards, letters and very brief phone calls were all I had to reassure me that my two dearest friends from high school were still alive and well.

I remember, attending Frank's graduation, which was a week after my own, being amazed at the large campus. The beauty of the architecture did not stave off the ugliness of the nearby neighborhood with its depleted buildings and vagrants sleeping under scaffolds or on park benches. The campus and city's cultural mix was intriguing and reminded me of that television show where you have all these strangers living in one house. I always thought, though the chance to be seen on TV was the stated prize, somewhere they had to be paying those folks some hard cash to live with each other. I mean, really, what's that all about?

His parents and I helped Frank pack for his return trip home. The summer was slow due to the many folks who had chosen to relocate immediately after graduation. Some had never even bothered to come to get their stuff. By mid-summer, Frank began to grow weary of our calm and safe surroundings. Fishing on the lake did not quench his thirst. Of the many jobs posted at the library, post office and small businesses, none interested him. He refused to take a job for fear the commitment would ground him and halt his so-called progress. All he cared about was finding a job in some big city.

One thing I could not share was his depressed state. I was, after only two years of employment, manager of Touffé. One day while he was visiting my home, Sarah called and invited us to come and celebrate her new job and apartment in Pennsylvania. She had planned on going west for the summer to be with her folks, but she had to attend summer school because of the credits she lost after transferring.

I declined because I had responsibilities. Getting hired at Touffé is hard. So imagine becoming manager. Four people were interviewed for the spot. The owner confided that he chose me because of my commitment to living and dying here in this town.

Frank went to Sarah's and stayed longer than expected. When he came back, I could read his guilt, by the way he bent his left knee when he spoke of the trip. Then he started fishing around about my feelings for Sarah. The nerve of that slut. To sleep with my best friend, a guy she knew since she was a mere toddler. I guess that's why I never dwelled on her parting. In the past, her prodding that I should go visit Frank because he was part of my history, part of me, made me realize she never considered herself such a part. Looking back, I failed to see how she used her dependency as strength. She clung to me as if I were dragging her along, yet she was probably anxiously waiting for the next ship to come sailing by.

I hoped Frank also saw this but he hadn't.

That summer, August brought the truest test of my friendship with Frank. After he left to go live with Sarah, I never called them. He rarely called, except for holidays and birthdays. His lone visit during that first year was to come tell his parents and me about his engagement to her. He wanted me to put aside our differences and serve as his best man. I agreed, then cancelled two days before the wedding.

We probably would have never spoken again if it hadn't been

for Martha. Frank was in town and I didn't know. His parents and I had not talked much though they would stop by Touffé and exchange greetings here and there. As I drove to Martha's house, I hoped that she would make the first move because of the awkward nature of our circle of friends, with every year bringing a new alliance and people in bed with someone new.

I yearned for that stare of hers, how it enveloped me as if I could live within her. But there sat Frank on the sofa. He was shocked to see me. I never did ask either of them what line she used to get him to come over and make the peace. The defeated look on his face, with the pursed lips and eyes focused on his shoelaces, told me that something was missing in his life, perhaps the comfort of home.

That look broke the ice. We sat on the living room sofa, unsure of how to begin. Martha guided us slowly. She spoke of the joy she had for teaching, the high school and its teams, what type of year they were having. The football and basketball teams were in contention for another state championship. Then she eased the conversation to the place we felt most comfortable, Touffé. Ever since becoming the manager, I tried not to come on my nights off, for fear the staff would think I was checking up on them. Unlike prior times, we sat secluded in the corner with my back turned to the action, most of which was Frank telling us about his life.

After a night of drinks and remembrance, we headed back to Martha's home and parted on good terms, by hugging each other and wishing Frank a safe journey back.

The last time I saw or heard from Frank was this past July. He came into town for a weekend's rest. The timing was odd because it was the third week of July, and he had missed the Independence Day holiday celebrations. Were it not for the fact that he brought his little girl, I would have confronted him about all he had done to destroy our friendship. He started by introducing me to Becky. I acted as if I did not know he had a child, even though over two years ago, Martha mentioned that Sarah had given birth.

Frank paced around the place delicately, adjusting chairs to pass through the aisle as if he was afraid of bumping into someone, though the place was empty. He commented positively on the transformation, the acquisition of more territory to include arcades and a play area with rubber floors, so parents could bring their infants and toddlers. Frank put money into the jukebox, as if settling when he could not find anything contemporary. I asked the kitchen to bring out his favorite dish. As we sat across from each other, he complimented me on the way I had maintained the place's integrity while expanding it.

"It was a hard task. The goal was to lower the age limit without alienating the adults. So what better way to do it than to make it toddler friendly. I am still trying to find a way to attract the ten to fifteen year-olds."

He laughed that knowing laugh of two lifelong buddies, then made a suggestion on how I could pull it off. The fact that he talked of something or someone other than himself meant something was troubling him. So I asked.

Though he knew she would not fully understand what he was about to say, he took Becky over to the play area, and placed her among the rubber balls and swings. As he walked back, I realized that he had gained the weight of life and his was the gait of experience, slow, careful and efficient. He sat then eased into the conversation in a round about way, somewhat remorseful, as if he did not want to hurt me. "Lately all hasn't been well in our marriage. Part of it is that I've had many flings during our four years together. I suspect that Sarah's done the same. The main gripe is that I don't believe Becky is my child."

My simple glance away from his mouth, with its predictable rhythm caused him to stop, so I could ask what I cared about. "Was Martha a party to any of those dalliances?"

"No. She's a friend of ours. Ever since Sarah, I haven't as much as kissed her. I care about her in a sisterly way."

"If you cared about her, you would have stayed here and married her."

"Why?" Had he been the dramatic type, he would have slammed his fists on the table, but he only got as far as raising them. He slowly lowered his hands and amassed another forkful of food.

"It would have made her happy. Would have made you happy. Sarah would also be happy."

At that point, all he could give me was some vague platitude. "Every house is not a home. You can live there because it is safe but deep in your heart, you know..."

"Is here home? Or the place you now live? Let me guess,

nowhere, right?"

Frank's stare was wide, and his changing facial expression meant that he thought he was seeing right through me, as if I was not even there or I was a stranger with a hidden agenda. "Just because you're scared to face the real world..."

"Real world? What is this fantasy island, where you come when your reality gets too stark?"

We sat in silence for what must have been an hour. Becky returned and broke our stalemate. Frank took a sip of his soda then extended his arm for a handshake.

We shook hands. Then, he began his walk out of Touffé. Through the window, I could see the sun fading slowly in the background, as it does at the end of a film, behind the mountains. Its color was no longer golden, but a pale orange resting against an empty sky. Frank opened the door, picked up a smiling Becky and placed her against the right side of his body, then turned to me. He half-smiled the words, "You know what Stephen? I don't know what life is about. But I know one thing. One's own happiness is not the first priority."

"You're just realizing that?"

With that said, Frank walked out of Touffé. As he turned to close the door, he stared at me while pushing the door close, delicately, by holding onto the doorknob and pushing it slowly.

# Touched!

They had been watching him for some time, but he didn't mind, not even in the beginning, when he first found out. Sure he threw the expected tantrum and cursed their god and their birthstones, but he hadn't minded. In fact, he found the whole sordid affair humorous. When he first felt the electronic gaze, a multitude of eyes observing his every move, he called Buster and asked him to come over with some assistance. During the visit, over a few marijuana joints, something he hadn't done in years, he contacted some old girlfriends to stage a weeklong fest of sex parties.

Vincent did this, because for the first time in his life he felt important. He had, through some calling, become the object of adoration, envy and perception.

The first week, he staged, in his apartment, the sex scenes to keep them watching, and to make them see how fascinating his life could be. Then, on the second and third weeks, he went on a self-imposed probation, no drugs, no partying, no sex, yet seeing women who wanted to break his vow of celibacy.

Those two weeks had caught them by complete surprise. Sure, they'd envied his hip lifestyle with women constantly begging for his attention, and the late night calls to be with him. But what intrigued them most, and made him the type of man they wanted was the way he handled boredom. This was one of the faults they had with James, the last one watched. This fault caused them to only watch James for two and half weeks.

Most folks when confronted by boredom searched for salvation of some sort: the company of a friend, the silver screen, or a trendy nightclub. But not him. He embraced boredom, as if it were a friend in the small entourage he kept. *Hi there, how're you doing B?*

He'd sit, for hours, with the music flowing, almost noiselessly, just loud enough to eliminate the dead air surrounding the conversations with himself. At times, he would talk out loud, about everything, from the formation of the universe to present day tribalism in American culture. He would talk, whether he was hungered or fed, sober or drunk, high or low. He would talk and they would listen. Listen to his complexity, then see him in the office the next day, and pretend they did not know that he possessed the same simplicity as them.

## II

He too pretended. Unlike them, Vincent's pretense was not a product of haughtiness; it was in the hope that he too, after being invaded, would join their little circle. That had been their intention, until month: 2 day: 7.

Vincent had grown tired of the whole act, and wrote a letter to his friend, Buster. At first, he thought of simply inviting Buster over, but the bugging had gotten so extensive, he felt there were cameras everywhere and knew his home and office phones had bugs planted to monitor his conversation. Though he knew the mail could easily be intercepted, it was his only chance. Since it was so obvious, he felt they wouldn't intercept a letter. In the letter, he asked his confidant, who'd been watched during his probation at another corporation, how to end the watch.

Buster did not know. All he knew was one day they stopped watching.

The previous month, Buster had suggested that Vincent confront James, the one who had come to his home and most likely planted the bugs. James was the obvious suspect because he was the first to befriend Vincent. He told Vincent of the ins and outs of the corporation, and the next thing they were having drinks after work. Their comfort level grew to the point where Vincent left him alone when it was time to go to the store and restock on liquor and ice. That's when Vincent figured it happened. Once he returned, James' quick exit after only one more drink made him the prime suspect. Still, Vincent hadn't confronted him, for fear they would make him out as a quitter or worse. He felt they would get upset because he knew about the watch all this time, and had, in effect, played and watched them.

Buster warned him not to let it go on too long, for fear they would become addicted to watching him. He did not heed the advice. Vincent wanted to—not win since no one really wins in this game—survive, to outlast at first, to somehow show them to trust their fellow beings without gathering every detail of their lives for inspection.

Then he wanted to outgrow them, to show them that their eyes were seeing more than three dimensions, and that they were experiencing more than seeing and listening. They were under his skin.

But in the end, he became the bug.

III

Month: 2 Day: 7

The surveillance had become part of his life, so much so that it changed his view of the world. He no longer cared if they were watching. He had always lived as a law abiding, socially conscious individual, but the duration gave the bug more strength. They not only watched his home and corporate life, but also his interaction in the home of his friends. Everywhere he turned, eyes stared and ears listened. It got to the point where two of the women's personal lives began to suffer.

One because he had, on day one, admitted lust for her because they were so different socially. The other, because she felt cheated she didn't have a man like him. He made her realize her husband's dullness. "Kathy, what do you really think of him?"

Kathy pretended not to hear by tunneling her gaze at the center monitor, which displayed three rooms of his apartment that were watched one at a time by simply touching a button. She was watching the living room, even though he was in the shower. She had grown so accustomed to his nude body that the empty living room with the small Panasonic television, opposite the plush sofa, tuned to Saturday morning cartoons was of more interest.

Rebecca glanced at the right monitor, the one they called "him." It was a rover. It was the last one placed. The camera watched from over his left shoulder, enabling them to see what he was watching.

It was eleven in the morning on what was the most beautiful day of the year. Spring had cracked the white shell of cold wintry days, giving off a large glowing sun with rays that bounced off mirrored sunglasses and car windshields. The rays were like the paint of an abstract painting. The glare possessed no boundary or true shape; it existed as if it were two young birds fighting for a piece of bread near the feet of an old man enjoying his retirement on a park bench. Their beaks seized the morsel, pulling at it from opposite ends; they were willing to share but unable because the bread would not, under any condition, split. And, the old man, in his serene state, walking cane on his right, with his hollow eyes hidden beyond the darkness of his sun glasses, pretends not to know of their plight, yet awaits the outcome of the struggle, with no interest in who wins, but only who struggles for the next piece he throws.

## IV

The following Monday he arrived one hour late due to a train delay caused by a sick passenger. No one questioned his lateness. He hadn't noticed the slight change. But as the week progressed, he began to notice their aloofness. No one discussed newspaper reports with him, or his view on last night's sitcoms. It was as if they'd stopped watching.

Did he care?

No, he did not. He had gotten to the point, whether or not he was watched, where he did as he pleased.

During Thursday's board meeting the five watchers decided it was time to discontinue the surveillance. Unlike previous endings, the majority did not want to initiate him into the circle. The vote was three against, and two for.

"That is totally wrong," said James, his tongue slinking deeper into his mouth to accentuate his point. James was seated opposite Rebecca at the round table discussion. "He did nothing during the regular probationary watch nor during the extension that should make him unworthy." James paused to gather his thoughts. "He, in fact, could teach us plenty."

"Teach us what?" Kathy responded, her voice bellowing a stern note, not with anger but a tone that suggested she'd grown tired of the long debate. "Week one: he's an insensitive playboy who 'cares' about every woman on a rotating basis. Weeks two and three: he secludes himself from everyone. And from then up until Saturday: everything is close to normal."

"What did he do Saturday?" queried the short redhead seated next to Kathy.

As if embarrassed, James lowered his head then mumbled, "He sat in his bedroom and cried for seven hours straight." Though James' watch was much shorter, he remembered when he first found out that he was being watched. Straight anger was his reaction; something which was totally different from his reserved personality. To James, Vincent's cry was his way of suppressing a stronger more profound anger.

"No sobs, just tears," added Kathy, her eyes peering at the redhead, as if trying to further convince. As if she alone had been the reason for his demure acceptance of pulverization. "Then he went around the apartment smashing every piece of glass he could find." She paused long enough to roll her hazel pupils. "If I didn't know better," she chuckled at the words, "I'd say he was touched."

The board meeting lasted another hour and would not have ended with a verdict had not Kathy made a believer out of James. The circle had the majority, but could not get the required minimum of three-quarters that it needed. James was involved on the whole procedure from conception to deception. When he became the object of their judgment, James boasted of his own ability even though they said he couldn't compare to Vincent.

But James didn't yearn for the comparison because he'd already been watched. He, the redhead, and Rebecca. Yet, he felt for her act.

"How can you two sit there, and claim you want him to know we spied on him? What if...if he doesn't take it well?" asked Kathy

The redhead sighed then chuckled. Though she loved Vincent's strength, breaking him was the nature of survival. This ensured equality between the members of the circle.

Rebecca tried to reassure Kathy. "No one takes it well, at first."

"Becky, how can you even think that way?"

"People grow up! They rise to a level they can't control. They realize this is just business."

"I'm against it. I'm scared..."

"Scared of WHAT?"

"Of him, the way he thinks he can seduce any woman. And if I don't fall for his game, I'm scared he may rape me once he is part of the administration."

James laughed at the humorless notion, dissenting to the mere feeling Kathy was trying to impose as her reason for denying Vincent the opportunity. "Just because a man says he thinks you can give good head doesn't mean he wants to..."

She jumps in mid-sentence. "Just because he does the things we normally do does not mean that he's normal." Her words caught their attention. They paused as if they were mimes encased in a glass box that was proportioned barely enough to fit their bodies, and brittle enough to be shattered by the scrapes of a fingernail. Their ears touched the glass. The noise of the words pitched through the air-conditioned room at about a mili-decibel, bouncing from ear to ear, hoping to be caught by a sensitive one who has lost a sense of what it's liked to be touched.

V

They deprogrammed the monitors, and he was left alone. Their exit was abrupt and Vincent immediately felt the difference, as if their gaze had been stifling his breath. He lifted his head and looked at the other heads on the trading floor, noticing that his, at that particular moment, was the only one facing north. The only one staring at the seconds of the clock.

He then returned to work.

An hour later James emerged from the boardroom to tell one of the floor's administrative assistants to summon Vincent. Upon his receipt of the tap on the shoulder, his coworkers applauded him. Though they had no idea who was being watched, they knew the watch was on because it always is.

Vincent entered the room and sat in the only empty chair, opposite Kathy. The elder woman spoke for the first time. "Congratulations Vincent. You've been chosen, after a prolonged search, to be the newest field manager, filling the spot vacated when Mr. Judd became chairman of the board."

He smiled then said, "Thank you." They all clapped, more motion then sound. Then Rebecca rubbed him on his shoulder. Vincent did his best not to react to her touch. Though she had touched him lightly, perhaps wanting to comfort, he almost winced. At that moment, the pain he felt Saturday returned and its surreal nature had meshed with the reality that he was sitting next to them. Their eyes reminded him of the cameras he had envisioned watching him. Yet, he waited for a message whose profundity would explain why he had to suffer so.

The elder woman continued, "Before officially taking the spot, you must pass a chemical screening."

"What type of chemical are you searching for? Blood?" His sarcasm moved James the most and confirmed that James was not on his side.

"Mr. Sethlow, please!" Her tone was an attempt to demean and dominate. "Let's not become emotional. The test is mandatory. It has to do with the plight of society."

Kathy, with her hands clasped and fingers locked within each other, added, "The sooner we get this little matter completed, the sooner we can begin to work as a group. OK?"

"OK." Vincent flashed a smile then left the room, giving them the impression he'd compromised without even a promise from them to set a predetermined end to this game. However, they had picked the end of theirs without realizing they had yet to reach the middle of his game.

Once at his desk, he began to pack his belongings into his carrying case. The act drew questions from his co-workers. His response that "We, the administration, suddenly have a policy" was measured to avoid showing his anger and disgust. A few co-workers began telling that most watched persons never even got called into the room. They were simply ignored, to the point where they just broke down and quit the firm.

Vincent nodded, yet realized that entering the room was not victory enough nor was sitting at the table. As he made his way through the doors leading to the elevators, the redhead stopped him. "Hey, where're you going?"

"To my lawyer."

Looking shocked, she batted her eyelashes and insisted, "But, you have to go to the medical office for the test."

"Since I couldn't keep it a surprise, I think it best for you to inform Mr. Judd that I plan to sue over this matter. I will be back tomorrow."

## VI

Rebecca and Kathy were in the family room of Rebecca's condo. Kathy sat in the small rocker, across from the oval window. The condo used to be a church in the nineteenth century and part of the twentieth.

Both women were a tad drunk, and could therefore express normal emotions, those that don't usually surface when they are sober.

"I think about him all the time." Rebecca began, as if the room were a confessional. "Remember the night he did an hour-long exercise routine after not doing as much as a sit-up for over a month? That night I came home, and Bob couldn't even do ten push-ups."

Rebecca sipped her drink, as if hiding her shame. The room stood quiet for a short time. The television's commercial interrupted the serene state, offering a cash rebate worth up to $1,500. The light fixture flickered, signaling the existence of an equally negative force, as if part of the tranquility had traveled and exchanged places with another.

Kathy drew strength from the momentary darkness, and for the first time since the watch she shed light on her thoughts of Vincent. "After Vincent left today, I went to lunch with Luke and broke off our engagement."

"Why?"

Kathy frowned at her brow and mouth, causing her words to creep out the side of her mouth like the spittle of a seedy character. "Because Luke is just like Vincent. He doesn't want to give me the satisfaction. He can't admit his weakness to me. Everything's an act to him, Becky. Everything."

Rebecca stared, admitting she didn't know enough to agree or disagree, so Kathy continued, "Luke knows he doesn't deserve to be with me. All his infidelities are his way of wanting to bail out. Instead he mistakes my forgiveness as weakness. He is scared to think that I just like seeing him suffer and wallow in his guilt."

She placed her left cheek on the back of her left hand, and rested her elbow on the arm of the rocker. Her body rocked in the chair, slowly, back and forth. She wanted to stop talking at this juncture but she couldn't. It was as if she was contemplating her next move, seeking a prey. "Get your bong, and let's do some hits."

Rebecca complied with the request because Kathy had sounded so weak. She, to Rebecca, had dismissed the reclusive, secretive nature she'd taken since day one, when she was the first they'd heard him acknowledge. They had all felt equi-important until they heard Vincent say, "I bet Kathy sucks a mean one."

What made it worse, more amusing, was that he'd told it to Buster, a person who had knowledge of them, though they never knew of his existence. From that point and throughout the watch, they teased Kathy by calling him hers. The teasing held until they saw and heard Vincent tell a married, pregnant friend, "I love you like a sister." At first, his words melted their hearts, warming his nonchalant, melancholic, erratic behavior, gelling it into a cohesive body. But then he removed her blouse to suckle on her breasts while tears rolled down her eyes, and her palms pushed him away with no strength. He then whispered the words again. At that point, they knew he had a power that he was willing to yield. This power threatened them.

The two women inhaled the marijuana smoke from the bong, giggling after each pull, letting the chuckling be their words. An hour later, Kathy continued where she left off. "It's different for him. Luke has needs and urges. Whereas I have no needs except basic survival."

They laughed and smacked palms. Rebecca almost said that she was the same. But she remembers how on Day 3 of her watch, she just locked herself in her bedroom. Two days later when Kathy and the other watchers realized she wouldn't come out, they came to her apartment and convinced her it was safe to come out.

Kathy lowered her head, swept Rebecca's sandy-colored, shoulder-length hair from her face then gave her a soft, wet kiss on the mouth. They exchanged a knowing smile, and Kathy said, "It shouldn't have gone as far as it did. I should have stopped the union long ago."

Tears streamed down Kathy's face, one drop at a time, sliding down her upper to her lower lip, then finally disappearing under her chin. Rebecca squeezed her palm to comfort her. "At least you weren't as dumb as me. I legalized my union through marriage."

## VII

Mr. Judd eagerly waited for Vincent's arrival. He wanted to personally tell him that although he understood Vincent's appeal, he could not go against the administration. Vincent did not bother to wait until he finished his words. He simply left the room.

"Even as the firm's owner?" asked Vincent, storming back into the room, startling everyone except Mr. Judd.

"Especially as the owner," said Mr. Judd, keeping stride with the impartial manner he pretended to be conducting the informal hearing.

Buster who was parading as a lawyer with the ACLU salvaged the moment by asking, "What if Vince took the test and passed?"

"Then he'd have the spot."

James interrupted Mr. Judd and Buster, "If he could pass the test, he wouldn't be wasting time with claims that he's being treated unfairly."

"He may feel more secure about the test, if at least one member of the current administration took it and passed. A member of his choice."

"Mr. Sethlow?" asked Mr. Judd, searching for a compromise.

"Fine," said Vincent, not knowing what Buster had in mind. After a brief conference outside, he and Buster returned and picked Rebecca. Upon hearing their choice, Rebecca's face cleared of all the pink freshness it possessed. All that remained was the yellow flaxen surface, like that of a leaf that had taken a beating from a winter frost, and was now trying to spring a new life for itself.

Rebecca did not say a word, only nodded when Mr. Judd asked her approval. After the meeting, she conferred with Kathy and the elder woman. They devised a plan that had Rebecca receiving the elder woman's urine before the test next Monday morning.

For Rebecca, the weekend passed too slowly. She lied awake at night, wondering if they were watching her. At the slightest opportunity, she aroused her husband so they could have sex. She took showers at least twice a day, unable to enjoy the feeling of having been touched.

All went well on Monday morning. She followed the plan–wore a skirt and two pairs of panties. She entered the room with the nurse. All was going as planned until the nurse ordered her to strip naked in the stall, then to put on a hospital gown.

"Why?"

"Mr. Sethlow requested that the testing be done this way."

Rebecca did as she was told and entered the cubicle to provide the sample. After the testing, she went into her office and began packing her belongings without awaiting the test results. Packing was harder than she had imagined. She'd been part of the administration only three years but had become quite comfortable with benefits such as a private office, reserved parking and four-weeks vacation time. She was not willing to lose it, not without a fight.

She stormed out of her office, and in a fast-paced motion, as if zeroing in on a prey, approached his desk. She was set to shout her words, but seeing his brooding expression, she spoke in a calm manner. "I don't understand why you chose me."

"How can you not understand something you've faced on a personal level? Isn't your being universal?"

"I voted for you. And, I was not in control."

"No one is!"

She exclaimed, "Kathy is!"

"That's odd. I always thought we were all pawns in this thoughtless lark."

"If so, then why me?"

"You touched me. You touched me, damn it." Vincent walked away, leaving her to contemplate her next move, and thinking that she may be under surveillance. And if so, he was not sure if she would do as he did and act as if it did not matter.

# The Immor'al Minority

—·*day 3*—·

Desmond is seated on the sofa, with a cognac glass in his left hand and a cigarette between two fingers of his right hand. The living room is unlit but it is bright because of the piercing sun. The room's three walls are sparsely decorated. On the eastern wall, hangs a canvas; the painting: a sheath stands in the center of a blood-red canvas, and around it, encircling its periphery, half-closed eyes.

It is four in the afternoon, and the television is on. The remote control lies on the table, left of the sofa. Desmond finishes his drink and walks towards the television. After he presses the channel selector a few times, he decides to turn off the set then walks to the room's lone window. The window occupies the whole northern wall. Outside, the usual crowd of men stands, languishing on Wade Road.

—·*day 2*—·

Yesterday had been the first time Desmond truly paid any mind to the beggars. It was in the aftermath of the deadly shooting of one of the men from their circle. Desmond recalled the event, exactly how he felt when he first heard the news report. The words of the song came first. The song was coming from the car parked directly in front of his building, under his window. He felt the vibration as if the window would cave, shattering the glass. The song was what opened his eyes to his predicament. First, the instrumental played; then the lyrics accompanied the instruments–*Papa may have. Mama may have. But God bless the child that's got his own.*

As he watched from the window, he saw the procession turn the corner, two dozen young girls, teenagers, pushing baby carriages and walking, double-file and to the song's rhythm. The song had basically told him his mission. He had to save his soul.

Desmond had never thought them to be part of a circle. He never thought vagrants, like those languishing on Wade Road were part of the cult. He wished there was a way he could take yesterday back.

*—day 1—*

The day had been dragging along, the way an overheating car with a flat tire slows up traffic on the expressway during rush hour. He was in the third floor's copy room, an isolated corner where he could waste one hour by pretending to be working. One of his co-workers, a man who never said even a simple hello, entered the room and engaged him in a conversation. "It's almost time. Isn't it?"

When Desmond first joined the company, he thought that the

two of them would click, especially after seeing Tyrone in his monthly divisional meeting. Desmond pretended not to know him, returning the treatment he felt he had received. "Excuse me. And you are?"

"Tyrone Freeman. And please, no games. There isn't time." Tyrone looked out of the room, as if making sure there were no eavesdroppers and no one approaching the copy room. "Your girlfriend gives birth in two and change, right?" Desmond didn't ask how Tyrone knew of his personal life; he assumes that he'd received the information through office gossip. As if he had lost focus, Tyrone digressed, adding what seemed to be his personal message, "What are you doing with a white woman anyway. Brothers like you crack me up. Here we are fighting a class war, and the next thing you know, someone like you shows up wanting to make a racial statement."

Desmond took in Tyrone's slender, weak-looking frame, thinking how easy it would be to pin him down and just mash him. Two things made him continue the conversation. First, they were in the office. And secondly, Tyrone had spoken using a familiar code, starting the conversation with the words, *what are you.* Questioning a person's being was the easiest yet ultimate symbol of recognition.

Desmond decided to answer, yet wondered why Tyrone wanted to know him now. "Love transcends all."

"What's love got to do with it?"

"Life's not all black and white. There is…"

Tyrone interrupted him as if to say, cut the small talk, "The only thing in life that's black and white is the game board itself. Everything else, including the inner soul is either, or." Tyrone's words and how he was standing demonstrated that he was more than familiar with the code. Tyrone stood, with his legs parted and both hands behind his buttocks; his left hand holding his right wrist. Tyrone continued, "If it weren't for her putting in a word, you wouldn't be working here."

"What do you know about her?" Desmond stopped trying to control his anger. Being in the same cult did not give Tyrone carte blanche to the point where he could disrespect his girlfriend and question every aspect of his life.

"Could you live peacefully in her world, her neighborhood the way she lives in ours?" Since they skipped the small talk, he didn't ask Tyrone where in Mission Hill he lived. Plus, he often asked himself why Theresa insisted they move to Mission Hill, a working class neighborhood that has been fighting hard against gentrification. "For your safety and hers also, you should attend this meeting tonight."

"What for?"

Desmond asked like he wanted a response but Tyrone gave him a curt "I just told you" as he handed Desmond a playing card. "Normal meeting time. Give it to the person at the door. Tell her she's also invited."

The card was a face card, but not of a standard deck. The figure resembled the king of a standard deck, but it was seated on a mule and dressed in knight's armor. Below the figure, an address in fine print.

Up until he had the conversation with Tyrone, his evening was already planned. Leave work exactly at five. Get home, do a quick workout, watch the game. Now it was nearing six o'clock and he was still in his office, behind his desk, pretending to be working but actually taking sneak peaks at the card. He had used the internet to map the trip to the address on the card. The location was beyond the last stop on the train. It would take him to a side of Mission Hill that he had never been. So driving was the best option.

As he left the office and headed to the train, he thought more of his neighborhood. But on this night, when he came out of the subway, the neighborhood felt different. He lived on the edge of Mission Hill, on Wade Road, the most recent street to face gentrification. Those who had spent their whole lives in Mission Hill had committed themselves to making sure that outsiders, as they considered young professionals and other transients, would not take over the remaining half of the section.

He grew up in a town not far from Mission Hill. Most nights the three-block walk showed why his parents had worked hard and moved around so frequently. They always felt their neighborhood was getting too bad, yet never gave specific reasons as to why. They had used cliché like familiarity breeding contempt. They also feared him getting too close with their neighbors. It was as if they felt upward mobility had more to do with whom you married than anything else. Yet, when he came home with Theresa, they were not welcoming. Unlike his parents, her parents were fine with them being a couple. The Johnsons understood that they really had something special, that chance is the catalyst for change.

Wade Road and the other streets were empty. Desmond felt that perhaps in a year or two, the realtor's promise would come true; the neighborhood would change and the price they had paid for the two-story condo would really be a steal. He couldn't see how this change would happen since most of the neighborhood was public housing that had to be converted. It took the county's leaders two years to get his side of Wade Road completed. He found it odd how his side of the block consisted of new condo units and directly across the street were old buildings.

The number of lit rooms meant that Theresa was already home. He would never have imagined them as a live-in couple, though there was this instant connection between them the moment they first met. At first he took it as part of her sales pitch.

Nearly seven years since they sat across the table, he and his music partners on one side, and she sat on the other. She was a young associate at the public relations company where he now works. The album helped her make partner, though the sales were dismal. Instead of the gold that she promised, the album went copper. It had nothing to do with her PR representation. Their independent status coupled with their new musical style coupled with greedy distributors coupled with...Desmond laughed at how often he replayed the unrealized dream. Perhaps, meeting her was the dream. He recalled how she called him on one of his lonely nights, when all he had to keep him company was a fifth of Beefeater's gin. She offered lunch and some talk. They were both twenty-three and idealistic, yet fearful of what society had to offer. They watched Eyes on the Prize together, got heckled while they walked the streets, even when not holding hands, but neither ever asked too much of the other. Tonight, though, he needed her to come to a foreign land.

Theresa was not one to do as asked unless it was something she had already planned on doing. They had four major breakups in six years. The last time they patched things up she was living with some other guy. She eventually left the guy when he proposed, yet she turned down his offer of marriage, opting instead to live with him. He wasn't sure if she was joking, when she told him that if the baby she was carrying turned out to definitely be his child then they could marry.

While they ate dinner he explained that the esoteric nature of the cult had beckoned him, but she refused to accompany him. She used logic to fight what they both agreed was ignorance. She simply said, "Tyrone Freeman is nothing but a racist. He may cloak his concern as a class struggle..."

"Perhaps you are only seeing the situation in terms of race."

"If you want to go, you go ahead, but I know who I am."

Deep down he knew she was right, but he could not turn his back on the cult. His father demanded that of him; explained to him how the cult is a subset of our larger culture. Everything that he faced in life, he could relate it to a lesson from one of the cult's books. Since the cult had never asked him to be present, all he ever had to do was basically talk the talk, dress the part and walk on beat. He lived by basically quoting from the book.

As he left for the meeting, Theresa's face showed she wanted to either argue or wish that he would not go. It was twenty minutes before ten, so he did not need to drive fast. As he drove into and through the deepest parts of Mission Hill, most of the houses were gutted, like they had been bombed. They resembled the people, casualties of war. Their shells stood, and through their windows, he could see right into them, taking note of the emptiness. How their weight dropped to their knees, as if their internal organs were being pulled. Both the houses and the people were cracked. Both looked as if they had lost the war on drugs.

The cemetery was on the edge of Mission Hill and represented the official end of Dire County. It was like a fort, the only building that served any purpose. The house on the hill beyond the cemetery was the best looking house Desmond had seen in nearly three miles. He had seen it from afar and been itching to get closer, like a shipwreck victim seeking the horizon. A young man answered, took the card that Desmond had been given, then led him through a door. Three other men sat erect on wooden chairs against the wall, like patients waiting for oral surgery. He tried to make eye contact with them, but they avoided his eyes, abating any possible greeting or conversation. Ten minutes later, a bell sounded, and from an adjacent room entered a crowd of men.

At first Desmond did not recognize them, but then realized he had seen them for the past few months, ever since he moved into Mission Hill. They were on Wade Road, morning and night. They often asked for spare change, but he rarely gave, mainly according to his moods or how they asked. When he didn't give, the beggars would become rude. When he gave, he would receive a kind word or a simple "be careful out there" or "watch your back." Those warnings worried him because they sounded like more than just random utterances. He actually felt the beggars knew of some approaching danger.

The men smelled fresh. They usually reeked of urine or booze or both. They stared at him, with some nodding, as if to let him know that they recognized him and had been waiting for this moment all of their lives. He had never spent more than a blink of an eye on them, even when they cursed him. Desmond always saw them as they looked. Vagrants, bums, scoundrels, ex-cons, niggers, white trash...that's all they were to him. And there he was, in an old house near a cemetery, where they represented this circle's wisest members. The cult's book told of the day that beggars would become choosers, but what worried him was Tyrone's affiliation with these men. And, why Tyrone had him attending this meeting.

"Desmond Washington," boomed a voice. The sound came from the speaker on the corner but he could not locate the person speaking. All four men stood. Desmond saw that the other three men shared his confused look, as if to say, we are being made fools of. An elder gentleman asked them to follow him into the main room. The room was set up as a place of worship. The altar was on the northern side and had seven empty chairs. A fire burned in the center of the room. The beggars walked into the room and were now nude. They stood, with arms folded across their chest, and their backs against the wall. A group of people entered next and took a spot next to a naked man. Each wore a hooded black robe, encircled by a white rope, which defined their shape enough that Desmond could tell they were women. Some were pregnant, yet their eyes were half-closed, reminding him of the painting in his living room. Their eyes made the women look intoxicated or high from drugs.

A melodic hum rid the room of its silence. The other Desmonds seemed afraid, but Desmond was not scared. He had never attended a ritual, but he grew up listening to his father's stories and had read the book many times. The only questions on his mind dealt with the beggars, and how come they were in this circle, especially since the cult frowned on poverty.

As the six elders walked in, he noticed that four of them were women. He had also never heard of women being initiated into the Council of Elders. The elder gentleman who had led them into the room took his place between them at the altar and began the ceremony, "What do our agents have for us tonight?"

A new group of people entered the room. They were men and women of various ethnicities, wearing clothes that showed they were professionals in varying fields of industries. A woman stepped forward, "*Night of the Knights.* The women did not show." Desmond found it odd that he had never heard of their circle, and though they knew the cult's modern day protocols, they were reading from a book long resigned as the past. She continued the reading, "Labels is the state. Let the victims be chosen."

Tyrone walked into the room to the sound of applause. His five feet nine-inch, square-shouldered, boulder for a head, really slim frame moved quickly, as if he was doing his best to shrug off the adulation. His head and eyes veered counterclockwise from each corner of the room until he found Desmond's eyes. Tyrone's eyes met Desmond's then he nodded his head once, as if asking for calmness from him. Tyrone spoke the words, "Warrior! I am the sacrifice, upholding the traditions of the past, willing to be looked upon as a relic."

"Any dissenters?" After asking, the woman looked at each group, daring anyone to speak.

Tyrone approached Desmond, his gait exaggerated, the way one rescues the potential victim of a hit and run. Desmond knew to stay quiet; in his mind, this ceremony still did not have anything to do with him.

The elder gentleman stood and clapped twice. The low murmurs of the other attendees came to a halt. Lights dimmed as the elder requested, "Desmond Washington, step forward!" Instinctively, Desmond made a move but Tyrone stopped him by placing his right forearm to Desmond's torso, then gave him a sideward glance to further request his calm and quiet. Desmond looked to his right as the other three Desmond Washington took several steps forward. "Where are the women?"

The other Desmonds did not answer. They seemed oblivious to the question and the book these people were reading from. Yet, they had received word, somehow conned or convinced to come into this circle. The elder was playing mind games, showing Desmond how random his existence is, this circle's way of saying his life could have turned out differently. The sheer weight, the mere translation of their first name in the cult required them to have achieved or have lived in worldly fashion. This detection made Desmond realize that this perceived worldliness, his being with Theresa Johnson, was why Tyrone had invited him to this meeting. So, he knew to protect her and his unborn child, he had to disagree with anything the people from this circle wanted him to do.

"Why did the women not show?" The seriousness in the elder's voice triggered a memory. It was a Pavlovian response, and had him on the verge of speaking up. Using his peripheral vision, he studied the looks of the other attendees. Common sense told him to save his defense and energy for his own battle. Not even the near pitch-black darkness of the room could mask the elder's disappointment. By now all the elders, occupying the altar, were standing, anxiously, waiting for one of the other Desmonds to try to run out of the room, or for Desmond to speak up on their behalf. He knew that the name alone could not be the reason the other three were here unprotected. The cult required that all acts must be done out of reason. He concluded that the other Desmonds were guilty of some atrocious act.

All it took was a nod from the elders and total darkness fell upon the room. Desmond clinched his fists, raising them to cover his face, ready for a scuffle. The noise level meant there were lots of movement, like that of a bar room brawl. The body next to him had not moved; Tyrone's breath remained steady, as if he was forcing himself to remain calm and focused. Oddly enough Desmond started to worry about Tyrone, wondering how he could have gotten himself into this position.

Desmond recalled that on his deathbed, when his father passed on the cult's book and his legacy to him, he told him to never attend a meeting unless he was summoned and no matter the situation, never to read out of someone else's book. Tyrone's arm still held him back but Desmond could now feel the arm trembling. As the noise died down, Desmond could hear the signs of a struggle. Ten minutes later, the lights reappeared and the robed women held sheaths in their left hand. Blood trickled from the sheaths, yet there was no blood on the floor, or any sign of the other Desmonds.

He had heard of this circle, but always thought it to be a legend. *The Cannibals of Belief* was a rogue circle, long taught to be extinct. The members were the ones said to sit around the table of past remorse and quote from only the cult's original book. They regarded all new editions of the book to be pure heresy.

"Lead the sacrifice forward," ordered the elder gentleman.

The woman came toward them, reaching out her hand to Tyrone, leading him behind the fire. She motioned for him to undress then sit, blindfolding him once he finished.

"Desmond Washington, step forward and state why you are here!"

Desmond stepped forward but did not speak. The woman, thinking that he did not remember or know the proper response, came toward him, handing him Tyrone's book. As he shook his head to decline, he heard the people in the room whispering to each other. One of the naked men ran at him and punched him in the jaw. Desmond fell. He glanced upward at the naked man, whose penis was dangling as if he was set to piss. When he didn't react, the man spoke, "So, you're going to act like you do not know, and watch a brother die?"

"Buck, step away from the pledge!" ordered one of the elder women standing on the altar.

"I'd rather see him die than lose one of our bravest agents. I know most of you don't care because Tyrone's been an agent for only a year."

Everyone was quiet as if considering Desmond's death, but Tyrone spoke up, "It's OK Buck. It is my choice to sacrifice myself for this stranger."

Buck stepped away. But instead of getting up quickly, Desmond scoped the room. The whole scene looked like a low-budget horror flick, a room lit only by fire, with people wearing hooded robes, and an altar.

"Have you knelt in the face of oppression to get where you are today?" asked the elder gentleman.

Desmond stood and looked toward the altar. He thought of pretending that he did not know the code they were using but the sudden disappearance of the other Desmonds and Buck's punch told him that these people were willing to do whatever it took to get their point across. "No. Hard work and dedication."

"Did you ever bend your stance in order to be the subject of admiration?"

"No. Eye to Eye at all times."

"Why do you pretend not to know?"

Desmond looked around the room, "Never knew mixed

company to fight for the whole."

The elder gentleman was the only one to laugh. His laughter was not humor but more condescending, as if claiming Desmond to be naïve. "Desmond, you of all people should know that skin color alone is not the issue. I am sure you know that there is a certain value assigned to a person's skin color. That translates into arbitrary divisions of class. As a circle, we recognize sexism and racism, but class is the structure that holds the other lines of divisions together." The old man bent down to pick up a staff, steadying himself to step down from the altar. He spoke as he approached Desmond. "By now I guess you've figured that our circle is what the majority of the cult considers to be relics. Well, let me remove one more shroud of secrecy. Your father was a great man, one of our bravest agents. He left our circle a few years before his death. Planned to join a modern day circle. Said the world had progressed. You know, he did this for you, after you met her. Now we're offering you the opportunity to bring back his legacy."

"Perhaps, his legacy is that he left because the world had progressed."

The elder man frowned at the thought. "No, it hasn't. You crossed over, and in your father's eyes, you basically blurred this well-established line. But, he never joined another circle. Left his legacy in your hands. Had she come here tonight because you simply asked her, you two would have been elevated to this altar. But, look around you at the number of naked men! Black, White, Brown, Yellow–it does not matter. Some very old, some younger than you! This should tell you, we've been presenting this challenge on a consistent basis. And, some things never change."

"What is the challenge?"

The elder smiled, showing how he loved and lived to say this. "We operate on blind faith and one belief: at the breaking point, no matter who owns what, people believe in the good of one another. So the challenge is for you to have Theresa Johnson, the woman you have chosen to link your legacy, walk in here without promise as to the outcome. If she does, we'll close this circle. You have the chance to burn a bridge so few have access to. Are you willing to do so?"

It did not seem possible but the room got even quieter. Desmond could not believe they wanted him to lead them out of the past, thinking that the path he was walking could be the bridge between them and the rest of the cult. Yet, it could be a bluff. Or he could fail the challenge they had in mind for him.

He looked around the room again, this time making a point to look at the different faces and shapes to ensure he would, if need be, recognize each person. He focused on Buck's massive frame, huge like a pro-football linebacker. Buck gritted his teeth, further mocking and threatening Desmond. Desmond knew to accept this leadership position; the positive was that he could dictate this circle's philosophy. These folks were living in the past; they were relics reading from an imaginary revolt, yet from what he knew they have never done anything. The cult kept track of what each circle accomplished, and *The Cannibals of Belief* were never listed.

The negative was that if he failed them in any way, he would have them as his enemies, for life. He reached into the left chest pocket of his jacket, and pulled out a book. He turned to the page, as if it was the only page in the book. His voice trembled as he read their oath:

*"For whom I thrive*
*as if my life was taped*
*and not truly live.*
*The death of one*
*brings the presence of none,*
*and assembly of the fourth dimension.*

*From hence I step forth*
*as if I had never broken North.*
*I hereby add myself, another nigger,*
*to make this procession bigger*
*because I know one day*
*someone will pull the trigger."*

The elder gentleman pumped his left fist in the air then hugged Desmond. "Undress him!" Two of the naked men approached. The lights went out. Drumbeats and chants filled the room. Desmond was now naked and felt a bit self-conscious because the robed women were all looking in his direction. The elder gent ordered, "Pick a keeper!"

"I already have a wife."

"Not legally! Nor have you two ever been recognized as husband and wife within any of the cult's other circles. So, you have to pick a keeper within this circle, to hold your soul in case you die before your time."

"I cannot do so. When the child is born, we plan to formalize our union in another circle."

"Which? Hers?"

"We have not decided."

The old man finally let his anger show. "See that's the problem with her not showing up! You have merged our circle's legacy with hers and her family's, and you don't even know which circle, which side of the line your child will honor. The child must be of this circle."

The naked men dropped their left arms by their sides and shotguns fill their palms. They screamed, "Freeze!"

Desmond thought of diving to the floor and rolling for cover but there was nowhere to hide, so he simply raised both arms.

The elder gentleman warned, "Never raise both. Raise only the right hand to show peace, and leave the left by your side to symbolize the piece."

Desmond dropped both arms.

"Freeze!" shouted the naked men.

Both Desmond and Tyrone did as the elder had said. A shotgun appeared in each of their left hands. Everyone in the room knelt, except the hooded women. The elder began to close out the ceremony but Desmond interrupted, using a code known only at the highest levels of the cult. His father told him to use it, only in life-saving situations. It is a favor you cannot ask twice in a lifetime, unless you save someone else's life. "She knows not the plight of the many. The reasons of none."

"How can that be if she is yours and carries your seed?"

"The seed planted does not make one a farmer."

"But, what if the deed done is a mistake, and she decides to take without ever partaking in the struggle to belong to the creed."

Desmond hung his head low, answering, "All will bleed." The negative murmurs from the others in the room made him realize that everyone understood the code that he had been using. Though this circle followed the normal protocols of hierarchy, it seemed that everyone in the room could act of his own doing, some sort of structured anarchy. Albeit structured anarchy was an oxymoron, but in this circle it was a reality since they all knew a code reserved for those at the highest levels of the cult. Their fixed stares forced him to explain why he was refusing to pick a keeper. "That is not my intention. But, with her not being part of this circle, there's a good chance we may start a war."

"Only if her circle fires the first shot. And, that's why we've chosen you." The elder's movements showed that he wanted the most positive outcome. His palms faced upward, spreading out only to return closer together. "You've built this bridge and we're putting our trust in you. We truly expected her to come here with you. We need to know whose side she's on."

Desmond tried another tactic. "You are less than one percent of the cult's membership and have no allies. And, you consider yourself one of two sides?"

"Yes, we are one of two founding circles. None of our members has ever split to form another circle. Our circle is immortal. Even if the whole cult is against us, we're still the other side. It is a simple proposition, she either comes in or you pull the trigger. If you cannot do this, then Tyrone will persuade her to enter, in which case she'll become a keeper of our tradition."

Desmond looked at the hooded women, wondering if it was possible that Theresa was one of them. The best way to get a clue was by challenging Tyrone. By talking to Tyrone, he would tell her how he planned to play his hand. He turned to Tyrone. "You betrayed me."

"No, I am just questioning your logic," answered Tyrone. Desmond and Tyrone were staring at each other, as if fighting a duel, studying each other's eyes, seeking a mere flinch. Neither wanting to be the first to walk away, potentially making the other think that he was the lesser. "But what about the woman? Are you sure she's not the one who has betrayed you?"

"The woman can account for herself. She does not need what little protection you can offer. The child is the last part; it is the reality. I was a symbol of our cause before you ever realized there was a cult." Judging by the idiotic, shocked expression on Tyrone's face, Desmond could tell that he was just following orders, and really didn't realize that he could die for this.

Tyrone tried to pretend that he was not fazed by Desmond's answer to the challenge. "I hope the woman is strong."

"If I were you, I would worry about myself." Desmond paused to gather his thoughts, then using his right index finger, he jabbed Tyrone in the chest. "There are those who live outside the cult who know more than those living within it."

The others in the room laughed. One of the naked men grabbed Desmond's shoulder and said, "Be patient with him, my brother. Your father was patient with you. He prepared you for this initiation. Just thank Tyrone, for we would never have known you were ready, if he had not been brave enough to question whether you knew us."

Desmond looked at all the people in the room, taking in the multicultural, racial mix. As he put away his book, he answered, "I'm not sure if I want to know you people."

Everyone laughed.

The elder adjourned the meeting. "Come on. Let's eat, drink and celebrate!"

Desmond walked out of the room with them. Tyrone walked out last.

As Desmond drove home, a bit tipsy from the food, drinks and the countless hours of small talk, he saw the aspects of the cult that his father loved. His father alerted him that those were also the reasons not to attend meetings and ceremony. Becoming too familiar with others in the cult brought along this feeling of kinship when no true kinship really existed. Desmond felt that he had played it smart by not picking a keeper in their circle. Yet, he knew the risk of not doing so, he could lose his legacy, his soul. If Theresa had come, for his initiation, they would have automatically become elders, and not need to pass the various challenges to prove loyalty. But it was not too late to accomplish this.

No matter how quickly he drove, he made no real progress in lessening the time traveled. The traffic lights seemed to be playing against him, just as Tyrone had done. It was a weird situation to have these people, self-labeled relics trying to lead the whole cult forward. They blatantly operated as a rogue circle, labeling the last five decades of progress between the races, the sexes, and society in general as flawed. As they saw it, today's society and its groups of diverse people could never bond because too many bridges have been burned. The only true unity was to exist on the least common denominator, abject poverty.

The secret nature of the cult never allowed, except those who worshipped in the same circle, to know who believed and lived the same ideology. He didn't even know if Theresa had been in the room.

Secrecy and honesty were the highest requirements. Membership in the cult was easy to attain, with nearly one hundred million members worldwide. But only one million members worshipped within the club's seventeen circles. Though Desmond never yearned to join a circle, he kept up on the cult's affairs by paying his yearly dues, thereby receiving each year's new edition of the book. Each year, there was always an asterisk near one circle, *The Cannibals of Belief.* They were said to be extinct because their members attended none of the cult's conventions, yet they were always listed as active. Most cult's votes were sixteen, zero, one, with them voting and abstaining by proxy. They wanted him to become that proxy. But, he wanted to be the first to break the line, the point of progress between theirs and another circle in the club.

Desmond realized that this circle found compromising humorous, yet dreaded conforming. They were holding out for a better day. An hour after the ceremony, Desmond felt that they had not been outside of their circle and in the real world for a long time. Desmond's legacy would have allowed him to leave their circle without taking an oath to belong to their circle. At first, their agents—everyday professionals, yet living in the past— intrigued him. Then as the night went on, his thoughts went back to the beggars, how do they live, how were they able to attain the status of prophets, planters of seed. What had they learned or done?

Now, Desmond's first mission was to have Theresa enter, undress as he had done, and worship in their circle. He knew she would laugh him off. Yet, he could not tell her the consequences of not doing so.

Theresa was asleep, a little too soundly, not even turning over when he turned on the room's closet light. Not waking was her way of avoiding conflict. Normally, no matter the time of night, she would wait up for him. He did not bother to wake her to tell her about the meeting. It was his way of avoiding conflict. He decided it was best to wait until the morning.

*—-day 2—-*

When the clock's alarm sounded, she got out of bed to turn it off then returned under the covers, a bit closer to him. He had not slept much. On his mind, his mission of her joining his circle, and all the while wondering how long he had. Once the elder adjourned the ceremony, no one mentioned what had been discussed. Since their circle was not active, none of its rules and standards were printed or known. Tyrone had approached him at the last minute, the same night of a ceremony in which he was to be initiated. That alone told him he had to act fast.

Desmond rubbed Theresa's stomach and planted a soft kiss on her shoulder. He needed to know whether she had previously been initiated as a keeper, and only had himself to worry about. "I don't think you should go on that business trip."

"I will only be gone three days."

Desmond decided that it was too late to take the indirect route. "You should have attended last night's meeting."

She pushed away from him. "How many times do I have to tell you that I have no desire to join that circle?" She left the bed. "I was born in the cult. You were born in the cult. One of the things I liked about you when we first met was, like me, you did not need to attend meetings and have someone translate your history for you. The cult is in my heart no matter how apart I live from it. I know who I am. And, if we do decide to join a circle, it wouldn't be that one."

Secrecy prohibited him from telling her that he had joined. "That's what the meeting was about. They consider our being together and our thinking flawed." They laughed at the same time. He continued, "I agree with you, but don't you see that there are bridges being built or burned on a daily basis. And, your reluctance to join their circle, in their struggle, will make things difficult for us."

"There is no struggle." She reached out her hand, as if the reflex of his eyes opening wider and his head falling back had made her reconsider what she had just said. "Just be yourself. Aren't you happy being yourself?"

"Yes, but I worry about our safety and the baby."

"Did they make a threat?"

"No, but they are more than ready to defend themselves."

"Defend against what?" Her frustration showed. "Look, I can't live, bound by tradition and lore. If that was my way, we wouldn't be together. I, I mean we are..."

Desmond interrupted her. "Flawed. We have no foundation."

"As much as you'd like to believe that there is this system, this invisible force, holding us back, we really are just surrounded by greedy people with no teeth. The only way they can eat us is by swallowing us whole. To do that, they spit on us, breaking us down to a lesser compound, and once we are soft, soluble, they swallow us whole. Then, we are just another part of them, what we call the system."

Desmond had never known her to quote from the book. She didn't want to deal with the issue, which was uncharacteristic so he simply remained silent, listening for clues.

She hugged him, trying to ease his worries. "I will always be here for you."

"Even when you're away on a business trip?"

"Yes. One which I will be late getting to if I don't hurry."

Desmond grabbed her left elbow as she made to leave. "Don't

you see that you leaving is the problem? I tell you we have a threat against us, including our unborn child and all you are worrying about is what you see as your purpose in life. The system that you don't think exists has you believing that you are only valuable if you make other people rich, and give yourself a chance to eat crumbs at their table."

"Can we discuss this when I come back from my trip?" She looked at his hold on her elbow, her way of telling him to let go. She smiled to ease the tension. "Come, let's shower for work."

They showered together. Afterward, while Theresa finished her packing, Desmond sat at the kitchen table, finishing the omelet he had prepared. Her rush meant that she would grab food at the airport. By the time she came downstairs, the taxi was outside, honking its horn. He ran to the living room window to confirm it was indeed her cab. The sound of her heels, with its hurried pace confirmed she was not hesitant or worried about leaving or being alone. He accompanied her down the stairs, and after a short conversation, he kissed her farewell over the taxi's half-open window. As the cab drove away, he took in how she'd styled her hair, pulled back and in a bun, allowing the sun to shine upon her pale forehead. Her eyebrows were trimmed and arched. Her green eyes glimmered, as she squinted, trying to diminish the increasing distance. Her lips, covered with a peach-flavored gloss, formed the words, "I love you."

Desmond smiled and waved, as the cab passed under the green light. After making his way back upstairs, he dialed the office to give word that he'd be late. The living room was lit only by the sunlight. He sat on the sofa, lit a cigarette, inhaling and exhaling the smoke, wishing the tension he was feeling would, like the smoke, simply vanish into thin air. He used the remote to flip channels, searching for an interesting program. When there was none, he settled for the morning news. The anchorwoman was covering the national news. He switched the channel again. Still there was nothing else to watch.

The anchorwoman was now covering the local news. The first story was about the birth of a child born to a woman addicted to crack cocaine. Desmond was not concentrating. The telephone rang. He searched for the portable unit then remembered that he had left it in the bedroom. By the time he reached the phone in the kitchen, all he heard was the dial tone. He went to the bathroom to tie his tie. Except for his jacket, he was ready to leave for work.

As he returned to the living room to turn off the television set, the anchorwoman said, "This just in." By the anxious tone in her voice, he thought that she was going to announce something of great importance, like the president had been assassinated. Instead, her report was a complete surprise and much more personal. "There's been a shooting in the quiet section of Mission Hill. A twenty-seven year old vagrant was killed, after he was mistaken for a robber as he strolled the affluent neighborhood. According to witnesses, he approached a taxi that had stopped at a red light, and tried to talk to the passenger in the backseat. As he reached inside his jacket, for what turned out to be a book, the taxi driver thinking he was reaching for a gun shot at the man. The drive fired several shots, killing the vagrant and accidentally striking the passenger. The pregnant woman died on way to the hospital. The paramedics tried to save the baby but were unable. The woman has been identified as Theresa Washington and the vagrant as Tyrone Freeman."

Desmond fell to his knees and screamed, "Forgive me for I have sinned." His lungs pumped air to his mouth; his fingers spread apart from one another. Motion on Wade Road stopped as if a man had flown like a bird. And when questioned upon his descent, he was found to have the power of reason.

He looked up at the canvas his father had left him in his will. The painting, *The Watchers*, was how cult members confessed their actions, in private. In public, cult members never explained their wrongs; they just played the cards they were dealt.

Desmond's eyes slanted upwards, admitting the betrayal he had come to realize. The canvas did not begin to drip blood from the eyes of the watchers like the book claimed it would. The canvas stood against the wall as it always did, crooked, resembling an old drunk posturing against a wall; his left hand a scaly mold of mildew; his eyes a boiling pot of blood; the stench of his breath, superseded only by the sewery smell of his clothes, kicking a sour note like a tenor who's not in tune with the times.

*Papa may have. Mama may have. But God bless the child that's got his own.*

He ran to the window and watched the procession turn the corner, two dozen young girls, teenagers, pushing baby carriages and walking, double-file and to the song's rhythm. The song had basically told him his mission. He had to save his soul.

Desmond watched, replaying everything that happened after Theresa left. Desmond analyzed the clues.

*The change in her name to my last name meant they consider her my responsibility.*

*The baby born to a crack addict means my soul is out there, nearly lost.*

*But, the real Theresa Johnson is not really dead and neither is the baby she was carrying.*

Desmond finally realized it was his initiation, not hers. Her legacy was intact, whether it was in their circle as a keeper, or part of another circle. They had given him a new mission in life, stand still, protect and lead this circle. Perhaps, in time, he will gain influence to set his own agenda. For now, he would follow the expected course, knowing this circle is filled with people who are trying to instigate a war. They basically sacrificed one of their own agents, hoping to start that war.

*Papa may have. Mama may have. But God bless the child that's got his own.*

As the procession left the block, he knew he had no more than two months and seven days left for Theresa to come into the circle.

Since their clues had come from the television, he grabbed the remote control, and pressed the channel selector upwards. The television's channels did not go in that direction. Instead it went to channel zero. A message flashed on the screen:

> *In order to be superior, we operate on a lower level. Most human beings realize three dimensions. In our circle, we reach a fourth dimension. No matter what's on the tube,*

*remember the code—Since there is safety in numbers, the one who acts alone is the immortal minority. Don't ever forget the person. For yourself; hence for your people.*

Desmond sat back down, staring at the television, seeking out other clues.

—-day 3—-

Desmond walks away from the television. He had watched nonstop since yesterday, stopping only to use the bathroom and to get food from the kitchen. Theresa had not called. All he is sure of is that Tyrone is dead. Nothing else is confirmed. He could wait for the next two months and do nothing, holed up as if surrounded by enemies. But this circle acted out their beliefs too quickly. Yet, he is sure they didn't think that Tyrone would be killed. Or else they would not have sent him so soon.

His other option was to take his place amongst the men languishing on Wade Road. That is the safe bet, if they would allow him to do like all the beggars had obviously done, and simply pull the trigger. Then he could see how serious they are in letting him lead the course.

His first stop is the northwest corner of the room, the bar. He lifts a bottle of Jack Daniels from the shelf and drinks from it. His next stop is the kitchen. He turns off the two pilots for the gas range then he turns on the oven and all four burners. Next, he goes to the apartment's smaller bedroom, to get the double-barreled shotgun. He had hidden it in the back of the room's closet, never thinking the men on Wade Road would act so soon. He spins the shotgun around his index finger then clutches it tightly in his left hand. He smiles for the first time in two days. Desmond sits on the sofa, polishing the shotgun and smiling continually. After he finishes and feels ready for battle, he goes to the window and sees the beggars on Wade Road with their left arms by their side. They look more alert than he'd ever seen them.

The television shows a bishop explaining the shooting, saying that it was a simple misunderstanding, a case of mistaken identity.

The television's underlying text states, *But we know!*

"They prey on us. For no apparent reason..." Next a man in a sweat suit appears on the screen. The caption states that he is a reverend. His voice is very demonstrative. His lips flutter, like that of a large fish. His eyeballs are half-closed, moist as if he had been crying. He states that there will be a march into the neighborhood of the murder, "...and in the end we will have justice."

Desmond looks up at the monitor and says, "You don't want that brother. You don't want that." The words flash on the screen, exactly how Desmond had said them. He smiles and leaves the apartment.

As he steps into the street, all the men lift their right hand, causing their shotguns to materialize. To further prove he was one of them, Desmond motions them away from his building. Once everyone was far away, he steps off the sidewalk. He looks at his condo, smiling as if realizing its true value as the front line of an ongoing war between the haves and have-nots.

He pulls the trigger twice, shattering the window occupying the northern wall. The building's upper level explodes, as if hit by a bomb. Fire spreads to the adjacent buildings. Desmond drops his right hand to his side. The other men do the same. Their shotguns disappear. As those who had been occupying the other homes scamper into the street, Desmond and the men languish on Wade Road, and watch the block burn.

# The Canon of Loose Cannons

My father was that man, and my mother was the woman. They were both special people. In their own way, they were both set in their ways, which unto itself was their downfall. They were wrong to have me caught in the middle of their tug of war. Alone, they were the same, staunch ideologues preaching the same truth, but with different words. I remember my life only after age seven. Before then, I took mine to be no different than the other children I met in kiddie circles, where one or both parents showed a child off, thinking their child to be the most special thing in the world. It could be another child's birthday, but their child could upstage the birthday kid with a tantrum, wit or any other skill or act.

To find me before age seven, I had to look at the family album. There, I found my mother and myself. The album had me with both sides of the family, lots of pictures that were taken in various kiddie circles, but mostly it had my mother and me. On rare occasions, the three of us, my mother, my father and I were in the same shot. The only pictures of just my father and me were taken by age three. It was as if my father no longer had any use for me afterwards, and that I became my mother's favorite prop.

She was always smiling, showing pearly whites, straight due to braces, and pink gums. In those pictures, my mother smiled like she had no mouth, no face, no body. She firmly believed one should floss with every brushing, and brush at least three times a day. Flossing was a definite after each meal, including snacks. One thing I do remember was the toothbrush and the floss kit. In fact, there were many toothbrushes, two in the bathroom, and the one in her purse that eventually became the one in my schoolbag. The whole set would change every season. And where there was a toothbrush, there was toothpaste and floss. She was not partial to any brand; she preached equality, a fair chance for each brand. But, once a brand disappointed her, she never used it again.

My father knew she was about appearances and holding grudges before I did. Though he never stated it, he also held grudges and relied heavily on appearance. Unlike my mother, he pretended not to notice the failure of others. I never knew the degree to which he internalized his disappointments. No one knew. Unless you had been welcomed into his tool shed, you would just pass him off as another soul unable to cope with the travails necessary to eke out a living in this world. His words, not mine. My father would gladly share his wisdom with you, but you had to be willing not to simply listen, but to internalize his ways. Then pass it on. So I figured somewhere along the line, I had disappointed him. Somewhere before age three.

I searched the album for the signs but could not find any. The clues were there, but I was blind to them. Eventually I learned my father's beef was with my mother, not me. My mother's love was not for me but her way of fighting with my father. I am not saying that she did not love me. She did, but only the parts that were unlike my father. She wanted me to be proper, as she had defined it. I could tell they both agreed I should be highly educated and athletic. They never directed me as to what they wanted me to do with this proper upbringing, except use my intellect to make others feel inferior. At least, that's how I sensed they used their smarts, especially toward each other.

They wanted me to take sides even though I had no idea as to why they were fighting.

They would fight over the pettiest things. That, I could handle because they did so in front of me where my eyes could serve as a moderator. However, the fights that scared me and convinced me there would be bloodshed were ones after my mother had tucked me in for the night. She would threaten to cut his balls off; his retort would be that he would smack that smile off her face. One night, a few weeks after my seventh birthday, I could hear them walking through each room in the house, one following the other into a room then walking out, only to have the other follow. As they left a room, the last person would slam the door shut. Then I would hear something within the room fall off its perch. I was real scared, thinking they would come into my room. So I walked out.

As they came up the stairs, my mother trailing slightly behind my father, I stepped into the hallway and shouted, "Could you two stop? It's not right to raise a child in this environment." For a brief moment, they stood side by side, paused long enough to look each other in the eye, then turned to me. They cussed me with the foulest language I had ever heard, telling me to shut up, mind my own business and stay out of grown folks ways.

## II

The schoolyard was a battle zone. Though I made friends easily, I knew they were the wrong kind of friends. At their homes, the parents would gloat over me, as if wishing that I, too or alone, were their child. It happened in each of my friends' homes. At first, I thought it was normal, sort of like etiquette. Then I realized my parents never did the same to the friends I brought over to the house. Neither ever objected to my hanging out with a friend, anyone particular staying for dinner or sleeping over. They hardly remembered who was who, though they often knew the kid's parents since some of those same parents were their friends. I have proof because I see their pictures in the family album. We went to their homes as we pleased. Yet, those people never came by our house, unless they were specifically invited, like foreigners with visas.

Our house was lonely and stood alone, detached, a two-level stucco, gray and white fixture with black edges. It was the corner house so we had lots of backyard space and a great view of the comings and goings of our block. The block was a dead-end, and the kids played without fear of heavy traffic. It was safe and the fights that took place were mild compared to the schoolyard. When the neighborhood kids played, they fought. I had been in many fights, won some, lost some. My mother did not mind me fighting. Neither did my father. They understood it to be part of the ritual of growing up.

The first time I got into what could be considered a real fight was in the third grade. I was nine at the time and had just transferred schools because of high grades. I complained to my parents that I was surrounded by bookworms and nerds, and I preferred my old school, and being in the same school as my friends. Since I never complained about anything, I figured they would give in, but for once my father showed some compassion for my mother. "Don't give your mother a hard time! She's pregnant and has done a good job getting you to this point. We're both proud of you, and you should be happy for us."

He had said a mouthful. For a man who rarely spoke, even to his customers, he had articulated his point precisely enough to let me know what I had learned was not his doing. Yet, he was proud of me. My father had something to teach me and was waiting for me to ask him. Whereas my mother was quick to share her knowledge, he was the silent type. By simply keeping it a secret, he had turned knowledge into wisdom.

When customers came by the house to order their product, he never took them into the tool shed. He used the den as his office. It was the lone room he and my mother shared gracefully. He would let me watch as the customer gave the details and he took the notes. He rarely interrupted, making the person feel as if he or she was the expert. From there, he would bid them farewell. Hours, days or weeks, he would spend alone in the tool shed, carving wood, sculpting and forming it into shelves, cabinets, tables or anything the person wanted.

My father was good with his hands, so I figured after following my mother's advice and confronting schoolyard bullies without any specific instruction as to how to win the fight, I would ask him. As I approached him, I expected him to laugh at me, call me a mama's boy, or something to show his contempt for my not being closer to him. Instead he lifted my chin. As I shared my predicament, his eyes were far away, though they were focused on me. It was as if he were recalling a particular episode in his childhood. No, he said. It was nothing like that. He had never been bullied as a child. He grabbed my hand, as he must have done in my early childhood.

The tool shed had always been off limits. No one went in there, not even my mother. After I turned four, my father built the tool shed, deep in our backyard. My mother had encouraged it. Thought it was a good idea that he struck out on his own, since he had a hard time working for others. But, she stayed in the corporate world; she loved the perks and the stability of the salary. Money was not a problem for either. Both excelled in their careers, and whenever my father's business suffered a downturn, my mother subsidized his needs. What troubled my mother was the way my father had decorated the tool shed. Built as a cabin, small and compact, it was modern; it held a computer workstation, a futon and the most modern tools used to cut and sculpt wood. But the walls told a different story. Lined in no particular order were magazine and newspaper clippings: the assassinations and shootings of various presidents and other world leaders; various lone wolfs, lone gunmen committing heinous crimes— LIRR in

New York, the U.S. Capitol, post offices, work offices, restaurants and schools. The clippings were framed, as if my father took great details to find the frame that fitted best, in color and size.

Once in my father's tool shed I knew I had made a mistake, the second of my life. I had forgotten what I learned at age seven, not to step in between my parents while they jockeyed for position, even though they had the same agenda.

My father was silent while he worked. He was typing some notes on the computer and edged me, with the slight motions of his hands, his fingertips beckoning me to speak. As I explained that the kids in this new school were not only smart but also tough, he answered that he figured they would be. I then told of how my mother said I should beat up the biggest one I could amongst the group that was picking on me. He stated she gave me good advice and asked whether I had thrown the first punch.

That day I had. The day before, I was sitting with three other kids. Unbeknownst to me, they also had been picked on and were continually being bullied by the same group of kids. My father asked what I thought would have happened if I hadn't sat with those kids. I think I still would have been picked on. He agreed. Then he printed out what he had been typing. The page's heading was "The Four Components of Power," and the single-spaced lines filled less than the full page.

As my father saw it, the population had four components: the government, the military, the mob, and the people, whom you can also refer to as the voters. He wrote that it was like rock, paper, scissors; gas, liquid, solid.

So, when it came to power, the first thing to do is determine which type of power you were fighting.

*If you live in a true democracy, then the people have power.*

*If you don't, then the military has power.*

*If the government is a charade, then mob rules.*

*Always keep in mind, government alone never rules because that would be anarchy.*

After I finished reading it, he smiled and nodded his head up and down, until he broke into a fanatical laughter. My father's laugh was contagious. In that state, he became a different person, open, teary-eyed and hoarse. That night we talked until it was nearly my bedtime. When we entered the house, my mother rolled her eyes to the other side of the living room, to where the twins sat on the floor, damaging their toys. She made slight mention of my bruised face, not wanting to acknowledge I had made a mistake in listening to her. To avoid the matter, she told us dinner was now in the fridge and to microwave it ourselves. My father and I sat at the kitchen table, instead of the dining room. We sat in silence, communicating to my mother, very loudly that we were bonding.

### III

Though I did not sleep well, the next morning I was full of energy, early to the bus stop, barely able to contain myself in my eagerness to get to the schoolyard. There, I stood alone waiting for someone to approach me. One of my friends came over and asked if I was scared. My answer was a question as to whether he had told the teachers or principal that he had been bullied in the past. Nothing happened before class. As I walked into the classroom, I made sure the teacher saw my face, the swollen eyes, the bruised cheekbones, and the busted lips. She winced slightly, turning her head away because she knew that a parent had not done it. If that had been the case, she would have jumped at the opportunity to make a name for herself, to call social services and have my parents brought up on charges.

My parents were loving people who had been drained of optimism but still they tried to deal with their conflicting views. I was the state of their union. How I settled my differences with the forces that had defeated them would determine whether I loved them both, chose one over the other, or abandoned them for a new way. To change course is not possible for either of them. They were like two cars with no brakes, being driven by blindfolded people, coming from opposite sides of a single-lane dead-end street. Jumping the sidewalk would be an option, but there was the possibility of hitting a tree or crashing into someone's home. Then they would both die. My father was willing to die, but not my mother.

She had no reason to make such a choice. Her family comprised of prominent people. The family album said so. She kept her last name after marriage because it could open more doors than my father's last name. Looking at his album during the times he allowed me into the tool shed, I noticed how different his family looked when not juxtaposed against my mother's family. My mother's family wore casual looks of contempt for all that had made them. As the years passed and I headed into my teens, I flip-flopped between that look and that of my father's family. Though it seemed difficult, it really wasn't hard to slip into the right accent or inflection. I learned to appreciate being casual when dressed in formal wear, and being very serious though dressed casually.

My father's album told of the progression of a rebel silenced by invisible forces. His was easily identifiable– top of the class throughout grade school, team captain in high school, dean's list during his undergraduate years then a fellowship for graduate studies. He also had pictures of over a hundred women. You could tell the intimacy they had shared by the downward glance in the woman's eyes, where they sat when the picture was being taken or the fact that he was never in the picture with them. Look deeply, at the sunken right shoulder, you could tell at what stage of the relationship the picture was taken.

My mother always posed square-shouldered, upright, with a bright smile and eyes staring straight ahead at my father. To hear him tell it, theirs is not the past; theirs is the truest of loves, the one where you share your true nickname. Unlike other monikers, your true nickname is the one that you give yourself and tell only to your soul mate or closest family and friends. So if ever you suffer from amnesia or become a lunatic, they could whisper it to test whether you truly are no longer there, in their reality.

When they first met, they spoke of revolutions, and that's why my father fell for her. They spoke of revolutions, and that's why mother stayed with him.

To hear him tell it, she will come back to her senses, to the days when she called him Hawk and she was his Eagle. He said pregnancy did something to her; he blames the doctors, claims the hospital ingested her with drugs that made her fight him when he wanted to name me Raven. And that was the beginning of the compromise. Why my name is Rayvon! She simply calls me her Ray, of light, her sunshine. But it hurts him to know that they had their own code and she had agreed then grown old, become the compromises of the past.

So, he collects his clippings, gathers the dust of wood and keeps to himself, the memories of young lovers walking barefooted on campus grass, the morning after a rainstorm. They met as grad students. One, in architecture; the other in mass media; both debating philosophy, agreeing that change is impossible but that revolution is necessary.

After a few years, he realized that no matter how much he tried, he was building onto the existing foundation. She agreed but did not quit her job when he left his. My mother said they needed the money and used their code to fight him. That was the beginning of the end. At first, she cared that he paid no mind to me then she didn't. She thought it was best and so did he. He always told her that I was his son, and that she was only my mother. No matter what happens a son is always going to grow up like his father. So she made sure I got a good look at him.

During my teen years, she was scared of me though I was a very well-behaved teen who really did not do all that teen rebellion stuff. She feared because she did not know my father during his teen years. Wondered aloud whether he was passive-aggressive even as a teen. Her concern was that I should always speak my mind. I could truly tell she had forgotten the time they yelled at me to stay out of their way. Dozens of times, whenever I tried to open up to her, she would shush me and say, "Ray, always remember you cannot commit a violent act in public."

Later in the tool shed, my father found it funny that she would say that without telling me the rest. It was something they had discussed when disgusted about how folks reacted too quickly and irrationally when they'd been done an injustice. "First, you have to let it fester like a wound. Then, put salt and onions on it while your blood boils." Then my father laughed after telling me the second part of what my mother had told me.

IV

My father was dying. My mother knew it and acted as if she didn't care. I was entering my last year in high school and had lost my virginity during the recent summer. Sex was something that I could have done since the third grade after I became popular, but I waited. Being popular was never my aim. So I made sure the other kids knew this by always standing alone. Though I had tons of friends, each action was mine alone. If I wanted to sit with someone new, I did. If I wanted to punch someone in the face, I did. If I wanted to join a club or team, I did. So they knew I was free.

For my freedom, I paid a price. It cost me the ability to be predictable. Eyes watched me wherever I went. When I walked into a room, conversations stopped or changed. No matter where, I heard the whispers. The whispers were due to the screams of a fifth-grade bully jabbed in the Adam's Apple by my ballpoint pen, to throw off his equilibrium, to have him gasp for air, while a loose-band of kids that he once terrorized stomped him. Organized, these kids understood that our code, my parents' was simple: *One bird can fly but the flock must not migrate.*

Raven, they said, was their leader when confronted by the fifth-grader's crew. Raven got beaten up for them. But, it was Raven who came back the next day and threw off the next bully's equilibrium. As more kids took on bird names, you had a group of lone gunmen versus a large army.

Nearly the whole school had secretly united against the crew of bullies. The bullies never knew who would attack them next. They always had to be together, and when they realized the impossibility of always being together, they called for peace.

That's when I shocked all of them. I agreed to the peace and told them leadership is a thing of the past, and to never forget our code. Everyone lifted her or his small carton of milk and juice toasting freedom. *One bird can fly but the flock must not migrate.*

My father was proud of how I used my power, but he was dying, because he realized I was neither his legacy nor my mother's. Though I was of them, I had developed an instinct that allowed me to rid myself of their destructive inklings. For my mother, this meant very little because she believed in death by attrition. But my father believed in attacking the enemy at its root, the way one squeezes a pimple until it pops. And, he knew I felt the same. He never worried about the mess his action would leave. He welcomed death.

So, death's arrival made him more solemn. I could not tell whether he knew he was dying, until he told me how to save him. He never came out and asked for my help, but the way he nodded when I brought her over the house told me she was the one. My father never smiled at any of my friends, especially female ones. He kept a distance that could be best described as spooky. With her, he sat on the porch and sent me to fetch him a beer. When I came out with three, he reprimanded me for showing no decorum then apologized to her. Over tales of his first love during summer camp, he drank all three beers.

When I left to drive her home, he slipped me his camera and a crisp one hundred-dollar bill. Instead of the back seat of my car, I paid for a hotel room. My father did not know that she was not a virgin, but he did not expect her to be. Nor did he expect me to be her last. From being with her, he assumed I would start bedding whatever moved as he had when he was younger. He probably wouldn't have minded if she became pregnant. Somehow, anyhow, he needed me to be like him, and something about my girlfriend indicated she was the peak of that slippery slope.

The next day when I came home, my father had a mischievous look in his eyes. As he grabbed my hand the way he did that first time he'd led me to the tool shed, he giggled. I hadn't been there as often lately. It had gotten to the point where the scenes on the walls spoke a different truth to me than the newspaper's written words. My father wanted to hear those words, but I was not willing to take sides against my mother.

My mother had never asked me, but she knew that I was a virgin until that night. Every year after summer camp, she would look me in the eyes, the way she looked at my father when she posed for his pictures. When she didn't get the downward glance, she would fake some silly conversation. Days later, she would arrange lunch with one of her girlfriends and their daughter, daughters or nieces. Normally, the girls would be way past beautiful. But even before my father ignored them when they came by the house, I would know they were not the ones I wanted to be with. My mother took that as a sign of rejection and we, for brief periods, would drift apart. She tried hard to make me be like her. For she feared I would become my father.

In all conversations, neither blamed the other for what they had become. Both wanted to know what the words on the walls told me. My father was less than straightforward. He simply showed me his new album. I was surprised he still took pictures. There were so many women that I was hurt, to think he would share his infidelities with me. He laughed, not his crazed one, but a sorrowful chuckle. "Have you ever wondered why the twins are not named after birds?" Seeing I was not willing to play his games and I was backing out of the tool shed, he shouted, "I had a vasectomy after you were born. I knew I had created perfection. Perfection, my son. Perfection."

## V

My girlfriend thinks I hate her. She doesn't understand why I don't want to have sex anymore. The walks in the park, cuddling and presents are just not good enough. She wants sex, even if it's just manual or oral. The first time we were together, on a king-sized mattress, in a modest room, in a fancy hotel, she was wet for me. Now she is drowning me, because of her constant questions about whether I am being faithful, and her continued statements that so and so likes her but is scared to approach her because of my reputation and my flock of friends. I suggested that we break up. She cried because she was only bluffing. But I told her that "Being between two, her only choice is neither. It's like my situation with my parents. I've come to realize that theirs is a fake conflict. I live in a divided house, a democracy where no matter which side I choose, I am still the outsider. I have no say, no power."

A week before my high school graduation, I made up my mind that I was going to kill my family. I had struggled with the thought since September when my father told me he was continually cheating on my mother and that she had cheated on him. At first I told myself the idea was crazy, but then I started paying close attention to the twins, Bella and Gustave. The twins came into the family shortly after my tenth birthday. Since my father was not one to watch kids, they went to day care right after my mother's maternity leave ended. At times, she asked me to watch them while she ran errands, but she never expected me to be a full-time babysitter or anything. The twins showed me how my mother and I must have been together. She doted on their every word and action, and they did little stupid things to please her. Whereas I had found my father and had an escape, some sort of balance, I now knew the twins would find no such balance unless my father died and their real father helped raise them.

Even in the event of my father's death, I couldn't be sure there would be such balance. What my father told me was always privileged information. So, I studied my mother and the twins to see if she knew he was not the twins' father. And if so, did she know that he knew? Then I noticed little things were being said, probably always had been said, and had simply gone over my head.

I realized the twins knew because she would say things like "Go to your father!" and they would not budge toward my father. This last level of deception convinced me I had to kill the whole family. The only item to finalize was whether I would kill myself after I killed them.

This murderous feeling had come many times, but I always rationalized my way out of the action. We were such a dysfunctional bunch, and our neighbors' respect was out fear, not love. People feared me, and my actions were borne out of my interaction with my parents. Now, even the twins were showing signs they were going to continue our family's ways.

Plus, the twins annoyed me because they were loud obnoxious little farts. Throughout their childhood, all I remember was their yelling and breaking stuff. They seemed as intelligent as I had been at their age. My mother must have noticed me keeping them under watch because one night as she ushered them into the bathroom for their bath, she asked me to join her. While she bathed them, I sat on the lid of the toilet bowl exchanging little remarks with her. I knew she had a secret, yet she searched my eyes for mine. Her curiosity dealt with my girlfriend and how come she didn't come around anymore. I told her it was because I didn't want to have sex.

"You sure are not your father's son."

"Are any of us?"

She cut me a look, questioning whether I knew what I was talking about. After drying off the twins and putting them to bed, she knocked on my door. I couldn't remember the last time my mother was actually in my room, to just relax and talk. At times, she came in to communicate a chore and to let me know she was going out. Besides that, she respected my privacy. Tonight though, she sat on the edge of the bed and smiled at me. This smile was different. It was only half of her normal one. The lips stopped halfway up and halfway down, showing only the edges of her teeth. While she rubbed my stomach, she asked, "What do you want from me?"

Her hand was cold and as I removed it, I then glanced at the large diamond and the band on her finger. "To stop poisoning my mind like you have poisoned dad's."

"Is that what you think happened?" When I didn't answer, she told me to wait, and she'd be right back. I had never seen my mother's album. It must have been hidden somewhere in the house. Whereas dad had a tool shed to hide his past and keep his private thoughts, mom had to nestle hers into a crevice, hoping no one would stumble upon the images of her past. My mother had no life before my father. All she had was family and tradition, education and career; then came my father. Her pictures and accompanying words told another side to his story, the linkages, of how they were both descendants of religious fanatics who did not believe in God. They were both creatures of culture, worshippers of mythology who chose to ignore what really happened in the past, the immeasurable guilt of their creed. Instead, they focused on lore and philosophy, and I was to be the creation that gave them a new starting point.

"How come the twins are not named after birds?"

"Because even birds are not free. They belong to a flock! That's what your father fails to understand. He belongs to us!"

## VI

The day before I was to leave for college, I decided that I could no longer live with the tension of these past few months, of no one talking to each other. We were a family, and though I could leave this house to never again return, this was my home and I was going to broker a truce or kill them. My mother's look told me she knew why I was wearing a camouflage army jacket, black jeans and military boots. My father never turned from his chair but he knew something was up by studying my mother's eyes and movements. The twins sat on the floor in front of the coffee table, finishing off a jigsaw puzzle.

"Have we failed?" No one answered my question. I sat on the leather armchair to my father's right. He had to be first because in a physical altercation, he could still take me. To avoid startling the neighbors, I planned to stab my father with a knife, a nine-inch blade with a jagged edge. My mother was on the sofa across from the recliner where my father sat. The twins were on her right. As long as I was near the room's lone exit, no one would leave. I just had to make sure I moved quickly after stabbing my father. To get my mother moving forward, I would fake like I was going for the twins. Her maternal instincts would kick in, and she would come. As she stepped toward me, I would clock her with all my might and use my right foot to hold her down by stepping on her neck. Then I would tell the twins to be still, not to worry, that our parents have to die. I would then bend down and slit her throat.

My only fear is that she would remain seated after I killed my father, thinking that he was my only target. Not realizing that the writing on the wall is for all of us.

After killing them, I would ask the twins to come help me dispose of the bodies. If they feel an inch of how I feel about my parents, they will start to help. That is when I will mutilate both of them.

As I thought through this plan, keeping my left elbow locked on the knife against my rib, I could smell the early signs of a burning pot, and heard the rattling of the lid. "Is something burning?"

"Your father is making his famous gumbo." The twins laughed at my mother's sarcasm. My father made the worst gumbo. Not only did he put damn near everything, except the kitchen's sink, in the pot, he overcooked it every time. Every time, he would make it, someone would have to go turn off the fire because he refused to believe that the thing was burning. This time was no different. As I got up to go to the kitchen, he ordered me to sit down, stating that the gumbo was like a melting pot, and all the pieces had to cook all the way through, to their softest point.

Minutes later, the clanking of the pot's lid had become unbearable and the smell of burning eggplant and carrots clogged the air. I got up again and this time my mother ordered me to sit down. The twins were staring at me, silently asking, "So what you're going to do about it?"

Then, we heard the explosion! Everyone ran. They stood on the edge of the kitchen, as if afraid to go near the stove. My parents stood behind the twins. I pushed through them and went to turn off the stove. The lid had flown off, shattering the glass from the cabinet, breaking some dishes. As the smoke rose in the room, they stood there shocked that this could be the result of so much tension and neglect. "The writing on the wall says that we have to change. We have to change in order to live peacefully."

My mother put her arm around my father's waist. In turn, he placed his right arm around her shoulder. The twins cradled both parents' legs, shivering while tears rolled down their eyes. I wanted to go and be with them, but I was afraid to be that close to them because I still had the knife in my inside pocket, and still had not forgiven them for what they all had done to me.

# The Revolution Will Not Be Heard

I

Seth learned early in life that he should listen to his inner voice. So, he felt everyone else should do the same. He was turning three when the cat, blind in one eye, ran into the street; and the driver, distracted, bobbing his head to a mindless song with a terrible beat and abstract, vague lyrics that supposedly cause people to want to kill themselves, ran the cat over. So, holding the cat with its broken leg and guts hanging out of the left side, Seth asked his mother what he should do.

Jeff heard voices as a child and would wake up screaming, with sweat pouring down his body. The elders said he was running for his life and that he had to block out those voices. Those nightmares ran in the family. His ancestors have had them for generations. In the first millennium, the same nightmares allowed them to predict events. They were sorcerers, to some; devil worshippers, to others. Their deaths usually came at the hands of others.

## II

In class, Seth always thought he knew the answer and was always quick to raise his hand even when he really did not know the answer. Teachers began to favor him, and said that he added something to the discussion. Though students, some smarter than he, would snicker, Seth did not mind because he was listening to his inner voice. That voice had become his best friend. As he grew into a fit, handsome young man who excelled in academia and sports, he was always the center of the action. By normal standards, Seth could be considered aloof, as he dated best friends simultaneously, gave answers to exams though he knew the teacher had spotted him, and interrupted any speaker mid-sentence. His voice was so sure that others would listen. When corrected or confronted, Seth's gift of gab focused not on the specific or larger issue, but the semantics, the ability to frame a new issue. He frustrated his peers to the point that their love or hatred became moot.

Never having raised his hand and when called upon, even though, at times, the correct answer traveled through his synapses, Jeff just stayed still and would simply stare. It was as if those nightmares had become his reality. His stare was mistaken for various stances: defiant, ambivalent, or dumb. Though his grandparents, his guardians since birth, knew that he was intelligent, well-rounded and agreeable, they could not help him. The grands had learned, head bowed yet proud, silent with a slow walk was the only way their kind could live in this world. Though the world had changed and the opposite was now how to get by, they told Jeff to be that way. So he got left back, over and over, though he aced his written tests. Still, the teachers found reason to tell the old folks that he was mildly retarded. In exactly what way, no one could tell except the psychiatrists. The doctors along with the pharmacists were adamant that they could fix Jeff. First, they presumed that he was stricken by the normal illnesses: manic, schizo, A.D.D. So, they prescribed pills galore and these dropped Jeff's reflexes and numerous functions. Up to then, he would listen to the voices around him, those of other human beings. When he realized what they were doing to him, he rebelled. Jeff, not only stopped listening, he eventually stopped speaking. Everyone felt sorry for him, even the other kids, who teased him for riding the special bus to school, for attending special classes, for just being special.

### III

As the years passed, Seth grew out of his self-absorption and found that his inner voice was leading him to his true calling. His doctoral thesis was basic, had been stated before but had never been used as the anti-thesis to the coming revolution. In B.S. times, i.e., Before Seth, the leading scientists and world leaders were all aligned, rallying toward cloning, implants of any kind, and were basically one step away from converting the majority of humans into androids. The majority of humans were for it. Yes, science and its machines had simplified their lives to such a level that their only complaint was learning how to use the machines properly. So, they figured since they knew how to operate themselves, if they were given what the machines had, then life would become that much simpler.

Seth balked at those notions, said they were barbaric and unnecessary. A silence came over the forum where the final decision would be made. As he walked to the panel, on the eve of the end of Pre-Civil Society, he knew if he had been a lesser-respected person and had spoken up, they might have performed a lobotomy right there on the spot. As he grabbed the microphone, a nervousness that he had never known slid down his back. The cool singularity of the sweat stifled his thoughts. The momentary loss of his inner voice convinced him that his was the correct assertion. "There is no need to do all this. We have something the machines do not have. We have soul. We should simply encourage people to listen to their inner voice." Seth knew what all the leaders wanted and he detailed the step-by-step plan on how humans and all other living things on the entire planet could achieve peace and tranquility.

No more talking because it interfered with your inner voice and that of others. The message and signs were everywhere. No talking, not even signing! The new society became known as Civil Society and its rulers were called *The Learned Deaf.* TLD threw their support behind Seth. At first people thought the normal course was to use one of the established sign languages, but Seth said no, that organized language of any kind would invoke chaos because we would still have cultural barriers. Seth's plan had layers and it covered how to remove these barriers. At first, we would use email, two-way page, interactive television, music and books. Yes, television and music was allowed. The louder, the better because it helped drown out other noises and helped connect the many voices in your head into just one– your inner voice.

## IV

As the years passed, Seth's thesis had become a reality. No one was listening but somehow we were communicating. Technology had been abandoned except for machinery. The primary form of talking, as we used to call it, was a new language. InnerVoice Sign was not like modern languages because it had no set vocabulary, no definition. No one told the next person what the hand, leg, general body movements and gyrations meant. It was simply assumed to be true and coherent because it came from your inner voice.

As the years passed, Jeff, in large response to Seth's thesis, had been freed. The nurses and doctors in the psychiatric ward started to understand his wild body convulsions, and the meaning of the spittle hanging loosely from his bottom lip to his kneecap. They began to understand that Jeff hung his head low with his forearm on his thighs because he had been defeated. Like them, he was willing to follow Seth's plan. They didn't release him right away. His reintroduction to Civil Society was slow. First, he had to learn to use and appreciate the computer, the cell phone and the other gadgets being used to communicate. The cell phone gave Jeff the most problems because he remembered that people used to talk into them, even the hands-free model used in the student driver vehicles. Jeff did not understand why he had to press in a code to unblock his identity, wait for the caller to see his number (identity), wait for the beep signaling voicemail to sound, press whatever numbers came to mind until the voicemail stopped recording, then hang up. Didn't understand when to punch his number. Didn't understand why the person he was calling had no voice greeting. Didn't understand that he should not talk. So, Jeff assumed his stuttering and limited vocabulary was why the driver/instructor covered his mouth and looked dead into his eyes.

Those clear pupils inspired rather than scared Jeff. For when he looked in the mirror, his own eyes were grainy and vacant. He knew the anti-depressants had taken away his inner voice and his ability to listen to the voices around him. So, on his own, in the dark of his room, he would light a flashlight and under the blanket, in secrecy, he would read, enunciate and pronounce the words he planned to speak the next day. Books along with television and music allowed him to expand his vocabulary. He really loved reading books but got no recognition for doing so. He realized that people lauded him more for writing. No one discussed what others had written. People simply were not saying anything these days.

So, he had to find solace and acceptability by the only other thing that he could do. Dance! In public, he rarely danced because the others dancing around him threw off his rhythm. No matter how precise the beat, they danced off it and oddly enough, no two people danced offbeat on the same beat. Jeff never understood how they did not bump into each other. Whenever the hospital held a party, Jeff simply stayed against the wall, listening to the speaker. He was fascinated by the voice on the speaker. As he would drift off and reminisce about the music of his youth and contrast it to today's music of irrelevant dialogue, he would stop the negative criticism, for it dawned on him that today's youth was receiving its own message on how to start the revolution against this madness of listening to your inner voice. The message Jeff had gotten before he stopped listening and speaking: motivate for the cause, not the effect.

## V

The world. All living things and those objects that we had never glorified as living were in-sync. To the common observer and most learned ones, it was not obvious that the inner voice was really just one voice. How else could cars drive themselves, planes fly themselves and people walk, scattered as if plotting points on their own exclusive graphs? I mean, not one incident where things collided or people bumped into each other. I remember standing on the outskirts of one of the world's greatest cities and observing people looking down on their communicators, walking full speed. No one had to swerve at the last second to avoid bumping into another person. No one brushed shoulders. No one had to say excuse me. These things were actually happening but no one was listening, so they really could not see it. It was a tricky situation. If you spoke and no one answered, did you really speak? So if you bumped into someone but did not listen to her complaint that you had stepped on her toes, did you really do it?

It was as if the truth was being layered behind this screen that was recording life then replaying this new truth quicker than a person's eyes and senses could process the real truth. And, Seth knew this!! He also knew that in the scheme of things, "I" was the most dangerous thing.

## VI

Jeff never understood why Seth's picture was all over the place and why Seth's was the only voice that he heard. Didn't understand the concept of Seth being the *Universal Translator.* No matter what television show he watched or music he played, once he focused his ears past the distortion used to fool the untrained ear, he heard Seth's voice. He researched and learned that everyone had to apply for a permit to communicate using voice technology. After or as you are recording your message, it would filter through a machine. Jeff had never met anyone who received a permit, but he began to worry that today's real message was not getting out there. Everyone had become this machine, this voice.

Lately, when he read his books, in his mind, he heard the voice. Seth, he concluded as his grands had stated, was an evil spirit. Seth had everyone listening to his own inner voice. The sad thing was that Seth was saying nothing. So Jeff knew his mission was to have a chorus with Seth and find out if Seth realized that voice and thought had been separated. That voice and thought, if unrehearsed as a union, becomes the same thing, a situation wherein the whole becomes less than either of the parts.

## VII

In his return to Civil Society, Jeff knew the scam he ran in the hospital would not work out here. He could not act like he could not dance. No matter how much the music moved him, he could not dance and show that he had rhythm. He definitely could not talk, though he had mastered language. Hiding his voice was easy. As a child, he knew no matter how innocent, the words were not his. They belonged to the voices inside of him. Now it was different because he realized that his voice and everyone else's had been co-opted. His favorite past time, reading, once a junction of thought and voice on paper had become a byproduct of only voice. So, he tried music. Blocking out the words, Seth's voice, he found the beat too new for his feet. So, he studied the young and saw they had been co-opted. Recalling his youth, he could not conclude whether he had been co-opted. All he remembered was a drug-induced stupor. Society had locked him up because he refused to speak in a voice that was not his own. Then Seth came.

## VIII

"There was a time, in the not so distant past, to have so many volumes of expression created in the same sphere would have been problematic. We have now become so skilled in deciphering communications that we are able to consume, take in, so much information. What is great about this, the ability for one voice to reach millions worldwide because of mass production, mass marketing. Don't you just love mass?" Seth paused for the laughter the people expressed though they kept it inside. "Some would say numerous distribution channels are the key. But, what makes Civil Society greater than I ever imagined is one person's ability to produce a product that might only reach just one person." At that, the audience applauded in the new manner, finger snaps, but real low and slow. Seth, accustomed to adulation, simply smiled then continued with his weekly hour-long address– *Owed (ode) To Technology.*

Jeff listened every week though it was not required. It had been two years since his return to Civil Society. By now, based on his taping and studying of the speeches, he realized that other people were writing Seth's speeches. The speeches sounded the same, not because of the subjective "I" but because Seth was really saying nothing.

It was time to act. Whereas he walked the alleyways and side streets in order not to bump into anything or anyone, Jeff had actually mastered the walk– two steps forward, one northwest, two northeast, two steps forward, sharp left turn, sharp right turn. The dress was simple– just look like you are trying to be a teenager, caught in a time warp, or trying to look futuristic. He could have mastered the talk and walk long ago, but he was resistant to the idea that he could fit in by following another person's style and modifying it a bit, so it could seem like his own; he feared becoming a clone.

What Jeff hated the most was InnerVoice Sign. On the surface, Jeff felt compassion for Seth. How could he not? Seth looked plainer and stiffer than the common man. Of *The Learned Deaf,* he had the clearest eyes and was trying to pass their vacancy and lack of experience and vision as the standard. Jeff saw them only through the television, but it was obvious that they yearned for a new dimension and were screaming, "This is so played out." Jeff knew if he could take Seth's voice and its propensity for seeking adulation and acknowledgment, and add to it his own original thoughts, then the joy and pain that Seth was quick to share with the world would have a foundation, a form. How could Seth not realize that he had been co-opted? That this was not his vision.

## IX

Friday nights, *The Learned Deaf* gathers for two purposes. They celebrate their achievements while showing off their new gadgets. Their movements show that they are yelling, talking over the music, but you can't hear them. All you are able to make out is their demonic, vacant eyes that cannot see people are trying to communicate with them. As if in their own little world, their steps are isolated; their garbs, outrageous as if the wardrobe of live mannequins; their existence, somewhat cartoonish, pale to the uniformity we once feared if we had been converted to androids.

Their disc jockey spins tunes in no particular order, secretly seeking ones who are trying to instill new ideas. That is their second purpose: to stifle those who dare not share their indifference, their voice.

Jeff was not the first and he knew this because he had observed how other promising thoughts had been converted to a

GUICHARD CADET

mere voice. They simply disappeared then reappeared, speaking in this new voice. This was the day to do it, and the song to use. The DJ threw it in with no warning and it brought Jeff to his past. He recalled how the song always gave him hope. *Welcome to the TerrorDome* spoke volumes in this world and the DJ knew a true rebel would get off the wall and dance on beat and scream out the words.

Having never seen what happened after the offbeat dancers form the circle around the rebel, Jeff did not know what to expect. It always happened that the lights went out, quickly came back on and then the party continued as normal. Tonight, however, he experienced it firsthand; dancers bumped into each other like go-carts with two drivers, a joke that Seinfeld once said. As their circle closed in on him, he was defiant, shouting, "This really is about nothing." They pretended not to see him as their feet stepped on his, then another hit his shin, until someone jabbed at his right kneecap. Down he went, trying not to focus on the pain of the feet stepping all over his body and face. The lights went out. Jeff was not scared because he knew they would not kill him. His focus, Monday morning.

In the old books, Monday morning was the blues. They kept those books around to remind people how fortunate they were to be living in B.S. times, where one had a choice of which eye you chose to see out of. In these times, Monday morning was a happy tune, a piano being played by a deaf man; his smile, formerly a contusion, was now healed because he had seen others moving to his notes; his thinking, I must be good. *Finger snaps.*

Jeff had no bruises. They had doctored him up to look as if he was well, but inside he felt this pain, which was bringing forward this fear, of being on a stage, knowing this was where Seth held his weekly address and his forum had been granted though he had not converted. His thoughts were coming in the form of voices, many voices, and as Seth approached the podium, barely glancing at him, he knew that it was on. The cameras began rolling which meant the world was watching, and he began to wonder why Seth would have him at the weekly address, especially since no one was ever present at the addresses. His thoughts were running wild and Seth began to speak, but he could not hear. Jeff sensed that the cameras were only on Seth. So, he shut his thoughts down so he could hear. Still, he could not. Then Seth stopped speaking. He noticed a nervous twitch in Seth's right hand. The pause and silence caused the voice in his head, his thoughts to come back, "Think something!"

The minute he started thinking, Seth began speaking. Jeff's thoughts were scattered but Seth's voice was poised and coherent.

"In a fight, you simply cannot attack a person's eye." Seth continued delivering his weekly address. "There are many eyes in this world, and they are a person's most precious thing. Today we will focus on the most important ones, the first, the second and the third, better known as Individuality and Identity. Either of the first two can be what you are born with or what you seek. Finally, there is the third "I" which enables us to have Civil Society—Indifference. Indifference is learned. Think of it as immunity. Learned Indifference is basically diplomatic immunity." Seth

155

further italicized his point by winking as if cueing the watchers to clap.

"Some would argue that you can't avoid Individuality and that you are born into it. Others would argue that Identity comes first and that you are born into it. There is this greater peace that we want, and it can only come in uniformity. It cannot be found in the clash of egos, nor can it come from the cliquish pandering, which in the end are the same. We become Indifferent only after experiencing the first two I's and learn how unimportant Individuality and Identity are in the greater scheme."

Seth waited a few seconds then walked off the stage. A sudden darkness fell on the room, which unnerved Jeff. Jeff was convinced that though he had never claimed individuality nor sought an identity, he had been indifferent since his first thought, whereas Seth had been indifferent since his first words.

Hours later, Jeff got the courage to simply walk out and return home.

## X

Since Jeff was not able to watch the live version of Seth's address every day, his recorder had it as a regular recorded program. That Monday night when Jeff got home and played the recorded edition of the address, he was embarrassed to know that Seth's voice was speaking his thoughts. Realizing that he was not saying anything, Jeff realized he had become a learned deaf.

Seth also recorded his daily address and hearing today's words, he killed himself, for he felt lost because he had spent so much time speaking, he had not heard the revolution.

As written in the provision for succession, the voice that killed Seth would become the new figurehead for *The Learned Deaf.*

News of Seth's death spread quickly and people could not function as they had been. The word was that they had to find this icon in order to move into a new time, Greater Seth time. Finding Jeff was simple because he was the only one walking and doing the old style. The sad thing is that he did not notice the style had changed. When Civil Society saw Jeff, they thought that he was an odd ball. *The Learned Deaf* who still was not listening and only searching for a figurehead turned Jeff into Seth.

Civil Society became barbaric and they all wanted to have their voices heard. *TLD* refused to listen. So, the first chance they got, the uncivilized stormed the gate where Jeff was being kept. Though Jeff spoke just like them, they would not listen. He realized no matter the message or the speaker, these people would not listen.

They forced Jeff on stage, behind the microphone. They all spoke at once. They argued as to who should go first. Their thoughts were violent and their actions showed they did not care about Jeff. As Jeff walked away, he did so by doing the old style. They quieted and did the same.

# To Kill A Messenger

It was a cold day in hell, what he called Manhattan on those early mornings when he did not want to go to work. He went for several reasons though, part of which dealt with how his mother raised him. To her, a man, any male over sixteen years old, had to be employed to provide for his basics, that is what she deemed everything but the roof over his head. Jean-Robert was expressionless as he made his way out the door and to the bus stop. Living in a two-fare zone, in central Brooklyn, the bus ride to the train station was short. But some mornings, after waiting for nearly twenty minutes for a ten-minute bus ride, crowded by grumpy people, bundled up, trying to cover their very spirit, all Jean-Robert hoped for was a seat on the subway. The train would take him to 59th Street near the edge of hell facing Queens and Roosevelt Island, toward the water.

Pedestrian traffic was heavy like a stadium ten minutes before game time. Instead of a stadium, their destinations were skyscrapers, originally built with design elements that suggested creativity. But as the skyline became crowded, the goal seemed to have the tallest building permissible within the zoning laws. In hell, construction was an endless industry, whether it was office buildings, or jails for violent criminals, drug users and other nonviolent social protesters. Hell was crowded and the office skyscrapers were no more than weekday stadiums or jails; your disposition decided.

The job was only a three-block walk. The wind pushed against his motion and made him realize that his ski hat, gloves and goose-down parker was not enough protection. To get through another day and the end of this week, he would need a will that his own father had not had.

Grand-Homme, to whom he was a junior, preferred his middle name because it had been in the family, reserved for the first son. By being called Grand-Homme, the father enabled his son his own identity, instead of simply junior. Oddly enough, as he flipped his scarf around his neck and up to his mouth, Jean-Robert thought his father had determined who the son was to be and three years ago, when he realized his son was average, he simply left. His mother never confirmed the reason Grand-Homme left, but Jean-Robert knew his parents maintained a friendship and his two younger sisters benefited from some sort of contact with his father. It was him and his interests and demeanor that his father resented.

So, the cold, the eight by twelve room where he waited for the dispatcher to assign his first round of deliveries was just another test of his will. The dispatcher did not call him for another thirty minutes. On cold days like this, he did not mind that the dispatcher held back his deliveries thereby preventing him from making the day's quota and eventually the week's. He really didn't care about the extra change because his mother taught him not to stress money. Upon hearing him complain about his pay, when he got offered his first after-school job, Claudette said, "A little money controls man; man controls a lot of money."

By sixteen he had already taken a liking to working. Sure, he loved the extra change to buy things, especially since his mother's money went mainly for the house and his sisters. Working enabled him to be around folks who lived a normal existence, yet had done things to which he had never been exposed. The job he worked as a high-school co-op student impacted him the most. When he first got the news that he would be working for a Fortune 500 company, he was extremely excited. During his senior year, the co-op program allowed him to work one week and attend school another. There he learned two realities, he needed to attend college, a good one. So, he made appointments to the school's academic advisors, to learn the steps for getting into college.

The second reality was that the power structure had an idea who he should be. Jean-Robert never understood why he got placed in one of the company's internal mailrooms, instead of working as some manager's assistant, a true apprenticeship where he could learn a skill.

That co-op job prepared him for this winter. College had proven to be more expensive. Even though he was a special needs student who was basically getting a free education, the stipend only covered the basics so he had to extend himself by working at one of the school's cafeterias during the semester. Since the dormitories were closed in between semesters, he had to come home. By the second week, two days after New Year's Day, he could sense Claudette getting edgy. She made a point of calling him Grand-Homme to remind him that she now considered him a man.

"Grand-Homme Mondiale," called the dispatcher. He hated how the dispatcher butchered his name but he got to using his middle name because people continually called him JR or pronounced his first name Jean, as in the pants, and could not understand that the T in Robert was silent. He reached for the packages, making sure that he did not make contact with the dispatcher's hands or the parts of the package the dispatcher had handled. Grand-Homme felt the man was dirty and probably handled himself at least twice a day. The dispatcher had two rows of stain, overshadowing his teeth. Never would he be caught without either coffee or cigarettes, and food stain on his top. His beard was scruffy and he would have been better off, if he simply let it grow, instead of shaving once every four days.

Their contentious relationship began the moment he realized Grand-Homme was a college student and he hated to hire students, but this winter he was short on messengers. At first, Grand-Homme thought of outright lying because most employers shunned students, especially those who attended school out of the city. Instead he simply said that he attended City College. Still the man made sure his assignments were not enough to qualify for the bonus. He would give Grand-Homme one token for five or more deliveries. This particular run was from the base to 53rd and Third, to 42nd and Madison, to 36th and Lexington, to 32nd and

Fifth, then to 23rd and Fifth. From there, he was to use the lone token to return to base. He had the option of doing the run in reverse. The dispatcher expected all this to be done within an hour.

As Grand-Homme made his way out the door, cursing the slob under his breath, he'd already decided that he could pocket this token by walking back from 23rd Street, never mind the cold. That is how he got even with the dispatcher by taking a longer time and skimming the token as his bonus.

He stepped into the cold and immediately felt the coldness of the steel jutting out the towers being constructed. The building took a life of its own, but instead of being built, the skyscraper looked near death, like an emergency room patient lying on a gurney with his intestines hanging out. He wondered if the other people saw him as he saw them. They were, no matter the racial classification or nationality, mere serfs. The cold forced people to walk with bowed heads, ashamed of their plight after millenniums of work. Up and down the avenue, he saw them gradually taking their punishment. He strolled slowly, ignoring the time, contemplating how he could escape this predicament.

When he got back, he did not mind being reprimanded because the other workers paid him no mind. They were in his age group, and he sensed they resented him for being a college-boy and because he had no kids like most of them. On Friday, the dispatcher gave him a bonus and a pink slip, claiming Grand-Homme's problem with authority as the reason for the firing. Relieved that he no longer had to work there, yet upset because he was counting on the next two weeks of pay, Grand-Homme didn't head home, instead he rode a different train, to do some soul searching. At first, he avoided the stares or simple glances of the other subway riders, only examining himself for the answers. Then it dawned on him, as the train came out the underground tunnel's darkness and onto hell's bridge, he saw bridges on both sides.

The light that dusk produced had already faded into a starless night, and only the skyscrapers lit Manhattan. Below and behind him, he saw the cars stuck in traffic. Tail lights and headlights moving only to bring people closer. There were languages being spoken around him. People were moving closer together. Somewhere and somehow they had found the optimism to see life as a glorious game, and the planet as the stadium where it was being played.

He laughed so hard that everyone within earshot quieted, thinking that he had snapped and would soon act out. Grand-Homme did not. He just steadied himself for the train's descent into the tunnel, promising himself that he would always see the lighter things of life, and to get a job, real soon. His only requirement was that he would no longer work as a messenger of any kind, or any job where he had to use the side or back entrance. Though he had not lived during segregation, those signs stating that messengers had to use the side or back entrance made him feel as if he did not belong.

Next, he decided to question his problem with authority. His father always told him that he did not listen. What he could not say was that he had no interest in being a musician, athlete or whatever pipe dream his father had for him. His sisters would have to live up to one expectation: no babies before turning twenty-three, unless they were married. Everything else they achieved seemed like a bonus for his father's investment of having children. But his son had to become another person, one his father had wanted to become. Or one his father would admire.

Being a telemarketer enabled him to be whoever the person on the other line needed him to be. He excelled at that and had no problem taking instructions on how to be better. As the two weeks ended, he admitted to the manager that he was a college student and was willing to come home on weekends to maintain the job. He worked for them throughout the winters and summers, except his junior year when he received placement in a foreign exchange program.

Coming to terms with authority and appreciating taking orders allowed him to excel in school. Life, in general, had taken a turn for the better. Even women took to his cooperative ways. Telemarketing research taught him how to use *screen-out* questions early to determine how far he could get with a woman. It also taught him when to cut things short and dictated that every relationship had to end.

The most astounding change was his new view of Manhattan. It was no longer the place of androids and robots, soulless people who had become drones in search of material wealth. Instead he saw the place as proof that the world's population could achieve "the peace," of living side by side. The architecture had become another symbol of humanity's triumph. Until he decided to see that he was actually in heaven or very near it, he lived here and had never eaten Middle Eastern cuisine, or sushi; had never been sight-seeing at the monuments that people traveled thousands of miles to see.

Grand-Homme had rededicated his life to simply walking an oft-traveled path and trying to make the footprints more visible. This would be his contribution, so that the next person, caught in the quagmire of low expectation or the lottery mentality of chasing pipe dreams, would see a way out and forward. He volunteered in the community, never asking to lead, only to serve. After receiving his B.S., he joined a top research firm, and while quickly advancing toward the managerial ranks, he started studies for his masters. Those who knew him pointed to him and his smile and positive outlook as the model. Though the department's director feared that he would want either a raise or promotion when he completed his masters, that fact did not stop him from giving Grand-Homme all the top assignments. A few months later, with his M.S. and no promotion, as he left the job for a better one, he heard the whistle.

The sound startled him. He dropped the cake that his coworkers had bought for his farewell party. The bike messenger had made no attempt to stop at the red light, but Grand-Homme figured that he was in dire need of making his quota. That sound stayed with him, marking the day that things began to unravel. Had it been an isolated incident or had his new job not been on the same block as his previous one, the sound of the whistle directing when people can come and go would have died down. Instead, he heard the messenger's whistle the following Monday as he stepped out of the subway. Everyone on the sidewalk stepped back as if their stepping off had been a formality, and that they knew the whistleblower was going to warn them to step back. To get out of his way, harm's way.

After orientation at the new job, Grand-Homme learned there were factions at the new office. Even delivery from the mailroom attendants was politicized. Instead of dropping the mail in each person's office or creating a central place where each person would have a mailbox, each department was required to pick up the mail from the floor's mailroom then distribute the mail to its own members. The problem was that no one from any department wanted to be responsible for this task, not even on a rotating basis. So, the mail piled up until something of extreme importance was considered missing. As days passed, Grand-Homme could not function in such an environment, so he approached his director with a suggestion. His response was that in a perfect world that could work but since it isn't, Grand-Homme should do his own thing and let others do theirs.

The following month he felt that he had gotten a sense that the young man responsible for the floor's mail was a sensible fellow. However, the floor's messenger sneered at him and told him, "Do your thing and let me do mine!"

This new reality troubled him. It was like purgatory, a writer's description of purgatory. Everyday he would step out of the subway and as he crossed the street, he would hear the whistle. This messenger, the whistleblower was really beginning to annoy him. The only way Grand-Homme missed him was to be early or late, and that was the resolution—to stay out of the whistleblower's way. Furthering his troubles, this new office did not care for his smile and upbeat manner. He had faced similar people at the old office and other places he frequented, but they were usually in the minority. In this place, they were the majority.

That led to the nightmares. He was never one to dream, let alone wake up scared, shocked out of his sleep. As they became clearer, Grand-Homme would wake, in the dreamscape. The room had no walls. All he could see was the brightest lights. Next to him, she would pop up, as if she too was having this nightmare. Weeks later, he got past the part where they woke, and the thoughts turned into a dream. The other symbols he assumed to be the infinite nature of heaven. The woman's presence scared him because he had never stopped for love. His relationships had never escalated to the point where either party cared if the other left. The only one he could think of was Salya, with the pessimistic outlook and the caustic tongue. She was his shortest tryst, two weeks and one day. He simply told her a smile couldn't hurt, hooked up with her just to make her smile. She sat two seats from him his last winter at the telemarketing firm. He approached her only because she was a lousy worker and he wanted to turn her into a productive bee. At summer's end when they were both set to return to school, they exchanged numbers even though she had cussed him badly the previous month and continually cut him mean looks during her remaining days at the firm. She was a burned bridge that had not fallen. Salya, he was sure, was the bridge he had to cross in order to understand this new workplace. Parts of him told him not to cross her, that he had gotten off easily, and to stay out of harm's way.

He feared that she would no longer have the same phone number. But, the number worked because it was her mother's in the house where Salya was raised. Her mother said Salya had moved but she would deliver the message. To his surprise, Salya called back, "Why are you calling me after all these years? Please don't tell me that you have some disease..."

"No, Salya. It's nothing like that. I've just been thinking about you, and wanted to do dinner sometime."

She answered as if she hadn't heard him. "Do you still work as a telemarketer?"

"No, I am a researcher for this psychology institute."

"In all your research, what have you learned?" Not understanding what she meant, he did not answer. "Are you still all happy-go-lucky?"

When she realized that he was not going to give her the answers she wanted over the phone, she agreed to dinner. Two days later, she walked into the restaurant, the sway of her hips demanding everyone's attention. It had been six years since he last saw her, and she had gained at least fifty pounds. Throughout the night, she rambled while he wondered why he even called her. She still had the abrasive manners. What made the evening worse was her loud mouth and general bitterness about everything. After dinner, they went for drinks at a low-key yet smooth venue, but one where he would not run into anyone he knew. He had hoped, by now, she would have mellowed but she kept up the negativity.

Finally he could no longer take it and began to do and say things to demean and annoy her. Much to his surprise, she seemed to be turned on by his meanness. As they left, she asked, "Would you like to see me naked?" Grand-Homme was shocked to hear her ask him for sex so plainly and answered, no. "I remember when you could not wait to get me out of my clothes."

"You looked good back then." He hailed a cab for her.

"That's the first honest thing I've ever heard you say. Normally everything out of your mouth is like doing one of those surveys, and you trying to be jolly and all personable so the caller would not hang up."

Another taxi passed without stopping. "One day someone's going to simply shut your voice out and everything else about you. I just don't want to live that experience."

"You're just scared of something that I learned as a little girl." She stuck her hand out and a cab came to a screeching halt. "The person you could be and the person you should be are really not that different."

He shrugged his shoulders, as if to say, so what; then it dawned on him what she was getting at. "Sort of like, can take the boy out of the city…"

She interrupted him. "Perhaps! But to me you have to determine if you are really you. Or if you have become the easiest person to be?"

"What makes you think I am not being me?"

Though Salya held the cab's door and had made no effort to hurry, the driver did not honk his horn to rush her. "From what you've told me about your life..."

"I have made the best of it."

"No you haven't because you refuse to admit that shit is really fucked up." She paused as if waiting for his reaction to her cuss word. "Look, you have my number, call me. OK?"

Grand-Homme decided to blow her off. "I called you. Now, the ball is in your court."

"No, it isn't. I have never had a need for you." She enters the cab and doesn't even look at him as the car drives off.

The next morning, Jean-Robert Grand-Homme Mondiale was cranky due to another sleepless night, one filled with recalling his date with Salya. As he stepped out of the subway, the whistle sounded and Salya was still occupying his thoughts. To the outside observer, it happened so suddenly. To Jean-Robert Grand-Homme Mondiale, the motion was slow and calculated, as if a blueprint had been drawn and the scene had been rehearsed hundreds of time. As the whistleblower sped towards the changing traffic light, and the cars came to their stops, and the people stepped off the sidewalk only to jump back at the whistle's sound, Jean-Robert Grand-Homme Mondiale stepped back to the curb with his left foot. His right leg extended, knocking the bike and the messenger into the cross street's incoming cars. The cab had no chance to stop. The sound was thundump, thundump, as the taxi ran over the whistleblower.

The noise caused everyone to move at an accelerated speed. Jean-Robert Grand-Homme Mondiale stared at the dying messenger, his body gyrating, going into convulsions as if his systems had gone into shock. Jean-Robert Grand-Homme Mondiale did not know how he ended up face down on the street, with people speaking in foreign tongues and accents while standing on his back. He really did not care, nor did he try to fight back to escape when he heard them saying to call the police. Jean-Robert Grand-Homme Mondiale finally understood why, as a messenger of love and peace, he had to make war. He just kept looking at the whistleblower, hoping the messenger would look him in the eye. The messenger's eyes would tell whether he was enjoying life or whether he felt that he was living in hell.

# Ten Funerals

It was the new shot heard around the world, and again, it happened in New York. This time there were no cries of joy in one place and sadness in others. Perhaps there was joy amidst our sadness, and it was just that I refused to hear the giggles and the jubilee. I had come to believe that others felt my pain though I only felt theirs when their pain presented an opportunity to show how caring I could be. To live in a place and not care about the welfare of most of its inhabitants had become my reality. My cynicism and indifference had forged an impenetrable alliance. Years had gone by and I never questioned what I had truly lost. In a way it was the best coping mechanism for living in a police state.

Growing up, I had heard of the silence that adults spoke of, the one in which you do not criticize the state for its blatant hypocrisy or its inadequacy. They talked of who had disappeared in the middle of the night. They carried the memories like a torch in a cave. Their memories of doors being kicked in sounded like the recurring nightmare that I live, the one with the light shining behind my head, then in my face, when stopped on the highway. Of my life, as a Black man, there is this part of my brain that is constantly turning to look at my periphery.

I know of others who live this same life.

We were doing about seventy-five miles per hour in the dead of January. A still cold hung in the air, the remnants of a three-day snowstorm that had emptied the streets and highways of most people. They had sought solace in their homes, sitting across board games and sipping hot chocolate. I had been doing the same until James' cousin asked if we wanted to make a quick trip. So my brother and I got in our car and went to pick up James. I drove until we got to Harlem. As we left west Harlem, James said Jersey into the edge of western New York was the fastest way to Ithaca. Since I didn't know the route, I handed James the keys. The four of us did what most teen males did during a short road trip, talk sports, music, women and school. As he drove and we bopped to hip hop, I never thought about the innocence I would lose that night. When the lights flashed and the sirens blared, we worried then calmed ourselves, thinking we would only get a ticket. But, more squad cars, like six more, approached, and we were made to stand, without our jackets, on the naked highway, while they ransacked the vehicle. The police's blank expression gave way to their expectations. They had foreseen headlines with their names and pictures, stating they had busted a drug ring.

Our anger spoke very few words then slowly drowned to a silence.

Since they had found nothing, except the fact we were college kids trekking a friend back to his campus at the end of winter break, the police let us go. No ticket for speeding. The no-ticket part was what we discussed once we started driving again, mainly grateful that James hadn't been taken into the stationhouse or given a misdemeanor. Somehow, by the time we reached a diner, an hour or so away from our destination, our laughter had returned, if only to drown out our anger. As real, young Black teenagers, we never learned the law, the Fourth Amendment, because even its knowledge couldn't have protected us. We learned from *Roots*, back in primary school, that our first steps on *Pseudonym's Land* were in shackles; that our last moment would be an eerie silence, followed by frequent wails from crying families; and that any misstep between those two points could indeed be our last.

My brother had been the angriest of the group, for he was the oldest and most experienced. I remember being there when he learned to be silent. Nearly three years before my first highway stop, the biggest event for Black teenagers in Manhattan, a club called the *Underground* was opening. With stick-up culture in full blaze, only the daring made the trek to Union Square. We got there late and never connected with our crew. Back then, we always rolled deep, mainly for safety, partly because that's just the way we lived. Young Blacks always traveled in packs, even if wil'ing was not our intention. The other youths were our witnesses in case we needed an alibi or witness of our persecution. Within minutes after we arrived near the club, a melee broke out, caused by police, some on horseback. My brother and I ran, stayed close together, dodging into the nearby park, fearing the harm that could come from the dispersing mob. As the climate cooled, we lingered around the periphery, trying to get a glimpse of the place, wondering what could have started the bum rush. Then he rode in, on horseback, with boots and a helmet and bushy mustache, thinking he's the law for just us. His request was that we move; to where and for what, we did not know. I guess since our motion wasn't swift enough, he began to make a scene. As other officers approached to oversee the event, a short one, who looked like the kind of kid that gets bullied in the third grade, shoved my brother. For a moment, my brother clinched his fists as he spoke up. The next police on the scene pushed us away. As more approached, it seemed that some of the police were pushing us away for our safety, as if they knew things were going to get ugly.

To this day, if you ask, my brother will tell you the story, as if he lives it everyday, like a recurring nightmare. The truth is, it is buried deep into his conscience, perhaps as the source of his decision-making, the obstacle to trusting or taking risks.

At times, I take my silence to be a cowardly act then names start to pop up. Larry Davis. Eleanor Bumpurs. Abner Louima. Amadou Diallo. Patrick Dorismond. The list goes on, and it proves how brutal or plain deadly the silence can really be. But, time marches to a beat, somewhat distant, though it is in my heart; at times, the beat is rapid. I call it fear, but it's a really a war drum proclaiming that violence is the only way to break the silence. That silence and violence are two hands on the same body. Whenever I watch the news, I usually see this fact. The media and the police state calls international Black teenagers who throw rocks, terrorists; they call national Black teenagers who throw rocks, drug dealers. No matter the label, we, young Blacks, are parallel lines, prisoners of war being led to concentration camps. I hear the international war drum and choose to ignore the sound because their leaders sound so irrational. In their own way these international leaders are despots, wanting to return to a mystical past or be our new police. If given the chance, our homegrown radicals who cry we should return back to Africa, even if only in our minds, would be just like these international leaders.

Worldwide, every facet of our being has been co-opted then reshaped, for there is a fear I bring about that I have yet to recognize. Across the ocean we'd traversed nearly five hundred years ago, our counterparts shout down the place we reluctantly call home. Their violent acts shame us to think we should be doing the same. Only keen observation shows their muteness to their national plight is similar to our silence. Whereas they can shout into the wind at foreign leaders, they never whisper, "I hate you" to their home-based captors. But, as the world gets smaller, its turns could no longer hide the faces of those policing our every move, no matter how swift the media spin.

We had entered a *Brave New World* with the calendar stuck on the year *1984.* Yesterday's enemies became allies and vice versa, but poor people remained disenfranchised, no matter who televised the election. The edict in Haiti and similar countries had reached the United States: to speak up yesterday when your party ruled meant a knock at your door tomorrow, because overnight they had recounted the vote, and are now working toward suspending the Bill of Rights.

*Power to Oppress and Label Individuals while Trying to Instill Conscience into Society*, in other words, POLITICS was still about guns and butter that were liable to fall into hands with itchy fingers. So I knew to remain silent by shrugging my shoulders, and simply say "Black man move on! You gotta move on... Black man move on!"

I had gotten into the habit of going late into the office, nothing extreme, only like twenty minutes, but I stayed past six p.m. most days to make up the time. On this particular day, the commute to work was slow and people were leaving the train at stops that led to no direct transfers to other trains. There were no advisories on why we were experiencing a nearly thirty-minute delay. The Q train makes its way to Manhattan by crossing over the Manhattan Bridge, and as the train emerged from underground, elevating onto the bridge, someone screamed the towers were on fire. At that moment, the majority of passengers rushed to the window. From my seat, I could see the fire and assumed that it was like the fire the previous time the World Trade Center had been bombed.

I had grown this thick layer of skin that prevented me from feeling pain unless something was prickling at my skin. The train crossed the bridge slowly, as if either the motorman was shocked at what he was seeing, or we were tour-bus passengers viewing the ruins of an ancient city. As the train submerged back to the underground, we speculated on what could have happened. The World Trade Center had been bombed was our best guess. The heart of New Yorkers were so hardened that a fire in the city's two tallest skyscrapers did not really faze us. The other passengers just looked, some tried to use their cell phones, and the rest of us just thought about the workday ahead.

The first time I heard the noise, I was with my co-workers. After going through the building's security checkpoint and wondering where everyone was, I found people huddled near radios and televisions. As the news channels positioned themselves for the coverage, they continually replayed the only visuals and sounds they had: the second plane crashing into the tower, with the noise amplified. People called around to make sure that their family and friends were safe. The news showed people panicking, running, ash covering their bodies, as if the gates of hell had opened on us. Then what no one expected happened; the towers of power collapsed.

Though we wore business attire, we were stripped naked, silent and motionless; the noise had cracked our hardened hearts, and sliced through our thick skins. As crowds of people moved away from the epicenter, kindness being exchanged between strangers, the city of clenched fists had loosened, allowing people to emotionally drop their ambivalence.

A new stream of consciousness invaded my mind, a new line drawn on the annals of time. If the emperor has no clothes on, do we? Perhaps there was no emperor. My first reaction was revenge.

Despite my unpatriotic moments, like not standing for the national anthem during a baseball game, this was the place I live. I joined the people on the street and I advocated for violence, to join whatever declared war, so the culprits would never again dare. My initial reaction, if I would not defend home, then perhaps I was living in the wrong place.

As days passed, I moved through various shifts, including the conspiracy theories, but no matter the stance, I knew the role my silence had played. By not speaking my peace and not holding a piece, I had duped the police state into thinking it was invincible and impenetrable.

I remember the highway, Northern Virginia, heading back to Prince Georges County, Maryland, a short drive to my apartment. I was being pulled over because I drove a red sports car. Police told me I switched lanes without signaling. Have I been drinking or doing drugs? Did I know the neighborhood I just left was a known drug zone? The neighborhood I just left? How long had he been watching me? I knew then not to say anything and simply ask whether he was going to give me a ticket.

Then, there was the edge of Denver, coming out of the west, returning from a cross-country trek. Nice policeman, really, no joke; he asked if he could search my car. When I invoked the Fourth Amendment and said he had no right to, he agreed saying that is why he asked me. Again, no ticket!

There is this silence that I pass on and it will be my legacy. I do not mean by rarely attending mass demonstrations in which people make noise, say great things, yet rarely throw rocks. The silence is my coping mechanism, makes me feel as if I live in a glass house. I see it in advertisements with slogans, like "Get the red out!" and it troubles me. Yet I say nothing, only make jokes. I see it in our reactionaries who think they are revolutionaries, but are mere stunt doubles for our assassinated leaders. I see it in the court jesters who want to be king by dancing into the nation's hearts. At times, I see my silence as the greatest weapon, my link to others who know that the state is imploding because it cannot continue to fight the same war with soldiers who are divided.

Among us are two sets of police: the ones who live to see us die, and those who die to see us live. For on 9-11, when the Bravest and the Finest ran into burning buildings to save others and give themselves, I realized there are these ideals they all cling to, that they cannot achieve because they have grown quiet because of a morbid past. They are noble men who police to bring about peace, yet some only want to maintain order. The latter seek perfection, a world in which the masses just toil and acquiesce, not realizing that our silence is brought about by cynicism and indifference, allies that allow anger to boil, then one day to implode, transforming people into your modern day suicide bombers.

There is a death we need to bring about, a death we need to celebrate. For the alliance between cynicism and indifference has us repeating a vicious cycle wherein we cannot feel our neighbor's pain, yet we do not understand why some are joyous when we cry. The police state knows that what we want to bury is their notion of what makes up a perfect union. As we move toward this union, we have to lay old ideas to bed, forever. You cannot have peace when you monitor and uphold the wage gap, racism, sexism, materialism, refuse to pay reparations, imperialism, etc...

We can bury the past, and I felt that day was just a warning shot, much like that fired by police at an escaping criminal. STOP!! As our silence turned into a collective cry, we held hands and crossed this divide, truly believing this was our chance...to stop.

# In Search of Purity

<for the Shasta I saw transferring to the F train at Jay Street-Borough Hall>

The night was gloomy or was that his mood. The moon hung low in the sky as if only inches away from the avenue's tallest skyscraper. He had not seen daylight all day. His routine had become fixed. Today was the day that his routine called for him to wake up at four in the morning, prepare for work and not return home until close to midnight. To get overtime at his job, he had to arrive earlier than the normal nine o'clock. The first time he arrived at the office at six in the morning, he was surprised to find it as busy as it was most weekdays at noon. Paul wished he had the luxury of doing his overtime at night, past six p.m. He knew those who stayed those extra night hours only goofed off. He could tell by the fact that all work piles from the previous day were intact at the start of the next morning.

But, at six p.m., Paul had to be at his second job, four hours, five nights a week, then ten more hours on Saturday and Sunday. Full-time. No sunlight when he tried to squeeze in some overtime at his day job. The day job paid well and he actually liked it. Only four offices, corner ones, per floor. Each floor-worker aspired to one day have an office. It took Paul two years to get used to the environment of one hundred desks, each only a foot away from the other, with no divider. Behind the desks sat professionals, tops in the field. Old, young, varied ethnicities, it did not matter. All sat on the floor behind a desk. Each focused on his assigned task. Heads rarely turned, and if so, only to prevent stiffness in their necks. They had been transformed into automatons.

All floor-workers were hourlies. The company did away with fixed salaries, and bonuses were assigned to teams that met ever-changing and impossible to reach performance goals. Overtime was limited to no more than ten hours per week.

So, Paul added a night job! At first stuffing envelopes was a part-time thing. The job bored him but he couldn't quit because his circumstances had changed. Never knew how much the sun meant to him, until late Spring, when the sunlit hours extended until eight p.m. Spring teased like no other season. It told those who loved the cold that it would stay, and those who loved heat that it would come soon. Some days Spring would please both lovers. Its temperatures would rise, only to drop unpredictably. Gray skies often accompanied the coldness, the drop in temperature, as if embarrassed and saddened by its own heat. Paul thought of his life as Spring, a reprieve after a cold period, a launching pad into extreme comfort.

On his overtime days, Paul ate lunch at his desk unless the weather was extremely pleasant. But, today, he had no reason to leave his desk. Co-workers returning from lunch passed the word that it was barely in the fifties.

Oddly enough, the night was warmer but still the clouds had not fully disappeared. The humidity mirrored his energy level. All he needed was sleep, not a whole lot; he could never get more than six hours anyway. The subway nearest to the night job was a local stop, so he had to take the 6, then transfer to the 4 or 5, then transfer to the A train line. With all the transfers and waits, his nighttime commute back home never took less than forty-five minutes. By eleven-thirty, he was to jump into bed, but sleep rarely came by midnight. Only after his wife would talk of her day could he fall asleep.

His movements had become fixed, and his thoughts had also become routine. Those thoughts enabled him to walk through life with no real effort, yet ever so often, the thoughts of a distant life emerged. As he made his way down the steps, the reality of hearing an on-coming train caused him to switch back. Unsure whether it was his train or the one on the other side, he hurried, missing two middle steps, stumbling a bit. Exiting passengers made no attempts to avoid the turnstile Paul was trying to use. The people moved rigid and fast, their vision tunneled. Finally, there was a break in the flow and he passed through the turnstile. The doors were closing. She held her palm against the train's left door panel, ignoring the conductor's orders, not to hold the door, and to let go of the doors in the back of the train.

He slid through, as if barging into a room and yelling surprise. She didn't wait or expect a thank you, but Paul gave her a nod then the words. As if a bulb lit in her head, she turned around, with a smile and a glance, to take in his chin and jaw line, then his eyes. The car was nearly empty, with no more than sixteen people, but he opted to stand, partly to give his limbs the chance to stretch. Sitting upright all day was taking a toll on his back and knees. Nowadays, whenever he stood, he could feel his joints loosening themselves. He had feared that it was the early signs of arthritis, but his doctor laughed it off and told him to shed fifteen pounds. Two years ago, he played sports, jogged or lifted weights no less than five times a week. He sure missed his early twenties and writing down five-year plans. All that went out the window when he realized after a certain age or point in life, time was really an abstraction. Seemed that the world had progressed and life had become a conveyer belt—no, more like a baggage claim wheel. How had he come to this point? He felt like a programmed robot, rehashing a routine where he needn't think. His body had somehow overtaken his mind, to the point where he gets up in the morning without an alarm clock, showers, kisses his wife goodbye, takes several trains to go to a job he once hated, and does his job— all without a new thought.

He was sure his programming occurred while he was not thinking, bothering to steer his life in his desired destination. Society had progressed to the point where the consumer culture had taken over, and people did not value facts, only opinions. Paul didn't remember the time or the particulars, but the signs were not subtle. Marketing had become the most important science. People were encouraged to develop a product or service, and market themselves as a brand. The idea was brand new but it made complete sense since naming-rights had became the biggest thing, that and sponsorship. Nothing happened without a business attaching its name to the event. Still Paul did not pay any special attention to progress, even after businesses started paying people to name their children after the business or its products. Most scoffed at the notion, found the practice absurd. Still some complied, mainly for attention and extra money. The defense was that people were free to do as they pleased. Freedom of choice stated that if a man could sell his sperm and a woman could sell her eggs, then a newborn's identity could be co-opted. People have been named after other people or things. What is the harm in naming them after a brand?

As the 6 train pulled into the express station, Paul filtered back into reality and noticed a rarity for the nighttime commute. The 4 train was waiting for the transferring passengers. Normally as the local pulled in, the express would be leaving, or the express would not come for another ten minutes. His ride on the express was for only four stops so he stood, staring at the passengers, most looked like they were in the same predicament that he had found himself. Their eyes told that they were in debt to society, for once having no choice. Clever marketing had lured them into financing luxuries, mere wants, as if the goods alone were their personal Gold Standard. The only choice they now had, to become parents and when they became parents whether or not to give naming-rights to their child. Those who spoke out against the trend unknowingly trivialized the struggle, by using extreme viewpoints to make their argument. They argued that big business would then ask people, newborns and old, to brand their company's logo on their skin, somewhere visible—forehead, palm or the back of the hand. Again, the prevalent argument was that people could make their own decisions.

Amidst the protest against financial dominance and environmental erosion, was the battle against the cloning of any living species and the decoding of the human genome. The proponents and the opponents were far apart in their views, yet they shared the same method of getting their message to the public. Their marketing campaign, with its gloss and extreme focus on creativity, obstructed their differences, causing most people to ignore both camps. Finally, a marketing company, at one time an inconsequential player, sat the two sides down and got them to agree to a basic campaign that would join the two sides. The company then held a world conference with leading policymakers and scientists. Though no major issue was compromised or decided, they agreed to a common slogan and marketing campaign. The ads ran in all media. The individual commercials were muddled, but the slogan was all the marketing company wanted the public to keep in mind: "That's the beauty of life, human beings!"

The slogan was everywhere, billboards, print ads, television, but radio seemed to be the most effective. Musicians and sports announcers injected it frequently. Talk radio used it as both sarcasm and euphemism. Since people slept and woke to radio, the message became part of their subconscious. No matter how hard the company pushed for a new mentality, stating that the ads dealt with all levels of beauty, especially how you treated your fellow beings, beauty remained only skin deep. Businesses, scientists and consumers did not care. Products had to be pushed, and the message was a product. To them, the physical form encompassed daily living. Pretty, though subjective, was beauty's first criterion, followed by fitness, identified as shape and muscle. Fitness was, at first, a fad then the norm. If you were not fit, you weren't.

*That's the beauty of life, human beings!* campaign had reigned in on the mental and spiritual anguish that had consumed humans. First, the scientists gave birth to the first bio-engineered humans, and named the series: Perfection.

Next, scientists claimed to have discovered the gene that determined whether a person would be good or evil. The revolt against such folly was the most forceful. Everyday people stopped reproducing to combat the co-opting of their genes, the invasion of the clones. All the revolutionaries thought it was a great idea until Perfection reached puberty. When the scientists allowed Perfection to mingle freely in public, the revolutionaries couldn't resist the temptation to mix and mingle with Perfection. These cloned people looked perfect. Scientists under the direction of businesses were identifying the traits to create what these two stakeholders considered the perfect human. Perfection had all the preferred features of a normal human, but in moderation. Height, weight, skin tone, and other characteristics were kept at neutral levels.

Slowly coming out of his thoughts, Paul transferred to the final train, yet nothing could get his attention, until she jumped into the train at High Street. Her entrance was like glancing into the face of a stopwatch at the end of the race. Everyone, including toddlers, stared at her. She offered a shy smile as if acknowledging the beauty of their response. She was what the scientists had in mind when they created Perfection, but they had missed by not factoring the cleansing she had obviously endured. Purity was at least six feet tall. She was a Shasta. During his teenage years, Paul and his friends used Shasta to differentiate between male and female Rastafarians. She, who wore no more than a body wrap, was voluptuous but that was not her main feature. Purity's beauty extended beyond the physical realm. Her smile drew people in, but it was not flirtatious; its pull was like a vacuum cleansing the film that had clouded the onlooker's vision. Her eyes, skin and posture told that her life was not a routine, that her mind frequented different spheres of life.

She stayed on the train for only one stop, making the transfer at Jay Street-Borough Hall. All went back to normal—at least to the naked eye. Paul was perplexed. He searched the other passengers' faces to see if living proof was not enough. He had heard the legend of the pure beings, but this was his first sighting. Paul could not understand how people could go back to their routine, after experiencing these sightings, phenomena in their world, clues to a different path. This was, perhaps where he'd always wanted to go, not necessarily to follow another's exact path but a reminder to seek what he always wanted, because it was attainable. But, he realized that businesses and scientists knew the real beauty of human beings was that they were programmed to follow a routine. They would breed with Perfection, giving the clones a soul, the purity they needed to survive then to outlast real humans.

But Paul was not going back. That action had been on his mind for such a long time, but he never had reason. Yet, on the eighth month of his wife's pregnancy, Purity's appearance into his life confirmed everything he had been feeling.

From the first day that he met his wife, he wanted to save her. From what, he had not known. Nadine was standing at the edge of the subway platform like she hadn't seen or heard the news reports. There were people randomly pushing victims off the edge and onto the tracks as trains came into the station. That was his opening line! Nadine faked a smile, as if to say there had to be more because that was a weak come-on. But, Paul reassured her that her safety was his main concern. Their courtship happened over lunch, hot dogs on the sidewalks of Manhattan, dancing at trendy nightclubs, drinks at his apartment in Clinton-Hill, then love under the Brooklyn Bridge in his car. As the still waters of the Hudson River carried the rhythm of unity, their romance ignited a passion and trust that would scare your average mid-twenties couple. Paul always felt that was how his bachelor days would end, with a beauty whose life's goal was to simplify his. In their newlywed days, they worked hard to erase their financial debt, feeling that was all that they owed to society. Then, as they saw what life had come to mean, they decided they would abandon the old revolution and have children, thereby creating more real humans. The new revolution's mantra was not about physical confrontation. The mantra was that "Everyone's looking for a leader. Why do you think there are so many babies born everyday?"

Nearing two years married and only one month before parenthood, the training of a potential leader, Paul knew he could not go back. If he did, he would end up doing what all these revolutionaries did. Countering as opposed to really creating. Seeing Purity made him realize that she had achieved this level of being. There were these strings, invisible to the naked eye; and they had tugged Purity, if only for one night, onto a different track. The concerns of rat racers like him did not affect her. She did not fear the annihilation of her gene pool; she knew the scientists needed her, to look at her and go back to their lab, to really try to achieve the perfection they sought. Her presence told them that real human beings were already perfect, and pure.

Paul felt the pull of uncertainty.

The subway car had few passengers. As the conductor announced his stop, Paul thought of getting off, and going home to his beautiful wife and the future. But in his mind the future was a place with only two base colors, gray and beige. So, he stayed on board the A train. Minutes later, when he passed Broadway-East New York, he began to worry and question his destination. Yet he remained glued to his seat, fighting the desire to go back. His life had become so predictable that he felt it was time to stop his mind, his smaller, less adequate self to reproduce. All his mind did was repeat what it heard or have him do what it had been programmed. He needed this upcoming birth to be something new, very different from what he'd been seeing in the world, particularly the "big" kids of today. He felt the kids were secretly being fed something. Their size was affecting their aspirations and value system. In the past, people feared being programmed mentally. They had lost that fight. Now their bodies were being taken over. Paul knew his child would not be perfect like the clones, nor would his child be pure, for he had not experienced the mental and spiritual cleansing needed to enter Purity's world. So why be here? The fatalistic vision of the beauty myth had consumed him.

Last stop. The train arrived into a zone he knew nothing of, nor did he know anyone who resided in Far Rockaway. All he knew was that the beach was near, so he walked towards it, thinking about what he would do once he arrived. It was nearly two in the morning. The streets were empty, save a few cars motoring by.

The darkness prevented him from seeing anything, but he could hear the ocean, as if it were a living entity, its waves pounding against each other then tumbling onto the sand. He sat and faced the ocean. The emptiness of the beach allowed him to hear the water, its sound reverberating within Paul, a silent communication. It related the bleakness of life, and the fickle nature of existing. Hours went by and the urge to return to his life's routine was never greater than that of drowning in the water. He simply walked in up to his shoulders. As he turned to leave, he saw the apparitions; they were all different from each other, yet they possessed that quality the Shasta had. As Paul walked towards them, he could no longer see them. He thought perhaps he should go deeper into the water; perhaps, dip his head below for a brief moment. He felt that he could actually stay underwater, swallowing gulps, his lungs being filled; his body violently flipping like a fish being pulled out.

Then his drowning turned him into a swimmer, floating under the water, yet conscious of his surroundings; he'd morphed into a new being, able to also live under water, perhaps even outer space. His skin's color changed to a fading blue because of the near-death experience. His mind expanded because death was no longer something to fear. People, hundreds perhaps thousands, were nude and facing the ocean, as if worshipping the openness and the horizon. Paul returned to the sand, sliding through the crowd, looking for a recognizable face. It felt like a baptism, a washing of his present self. More than a bath, the water cleansed his doubts that he would never find what he was seeking. He walked away from the water's edge, blending in and making conversation with the other purists.

It took Paul a few days to become familiar with their ritual. They started the morning and ended the night with their simple creed, "Say a new prayer for the mother with the bloodied hands. Dearly Beloved, we are gathered here today to give birth to Purity. Rainbow-colored in body. Naked, under our creator, Space, the Sea. For the sharks of the old world have stripped us of our natural fiber. All in the name of material culture. May our children be pure in spirit, normal in body and fluid in purpose. To eliminate the need to be perfect. To maintain our diversity. To protect our personal freedom."

The purists live on the edge of the water, stand on the sands of time, and drown themselves daily. They are invisible to the tainted who come to the beach to simply splash around in the water. Once in a while the purists roam visible, amongst those seeking perfection. Those moments are for reclamation of people who were once pure but have become tainted by slumming in the material culture. The purists reach out to them, to show that life is a cycle, at times vicious, but continually evolving if they are willing to let their old ways die. It is the purists' duty to remain hidden, until people truly need them. Their journeys are for reclamation, to let the people know they are natural and they belong.

As Paul emerged from the water, the moon was fading beyond the horizon and the sun's glare was beginning to make its presence. His death then life amongst the purists had felt so real he could recall: during one of his reclamation journeys, his guilt had paralyzed him when he saw a young mother pushing a stroller. That he almost went back to where he felt he belong. But it had been years, since he last saw Nadine. His first days at the beach, he felt he should be home with his wife, working twelve-hour days, preparing to be a father. Often he wondered whether Nadine had a boy or a girl, and how she was able to manage without him. He wondered whatever became of the child. And wanted to ask about them, seek them out. Pick up the telephone and call to hear her laughter and joy about his safety. As she tells it, she had this sighting. Three days after Paul left. Of a man, who looked way past incredible. The baby died the first time Nadine drowned herself. But, the baby, she comes to her in dreams to say that she is well. That Paul should call so they can get together soon. To share a laugh about the past. Perhaps lunch or drinks, or holding hands under the Brooklyn Bridge. Propose a toast to purity.

Paul walked out of the water and thoughts of a distant life, realizing how far he had come. As he boarded the train, he took note of the people heading to work, their faces so serious. He did his best to hide his smile, knowing they would not understand why he is rejoicing. His cleansing was still too new to him. He lacked the confidence, to smile at them and have them seek his physical form for guidance. But, he knew the confidence to reclaim others would soon come.

His thoughts were like the train's motion. They were certain points during the journey that it rocked like a roller coaster, producing a fear of the cars plunging into the water. Then, as he took in the view of Manhattan's skyline and the airport, the motion felt like that of a plane landing. The water moved calmly and the train submerged under the inlet, picking up passengers and bringing him home to his wife. He knew she worried all night that he had not come home, but she would understand his explanation that he needed to clear his thoughts, to break out his routine and simplify his being.

## About the Author

Guichard Cadet was born in Haiti. He moved to New York in 1977, and received his bachelor's degree from the State University, College at New Paltz. He is a member of Kappa Alpha Psi Fraternity, Inc.

Guichard has been a participant in the Caribbean Writers Summer Institute, and has a MBA from Howard University. He is the founder of La Caille Nous Publishing Company.